D. A Shroud
from uncle Bob
& Auntie Dawn.
29.6.72.

PUFFIN BOOKS
*Editor: Kaye Webb*



Syla was ... ng, weighing ... rk brown she...

At first glance she was identical with the forty-nine other females of her tribe, and the cage where she lived was identical with theirs, except for one thing – there was a loose staple in the floor of her sleeping box. And that was the way that Syla escaped from the fur farm to find a new life, free in a remote valley on the edge of Dartmoor, free to hunt and fish and play, and also to face the dangers of traps or sudden chills or fierce animals, or the perils of the wild life which has no mercy on weakness or carelessness.

Ewan Clarkson is an expert naturalist and makes a fascinating story of Syla's year on the moor, her brief courtship with another escaped mink and her life with her cubs. At the same time he tells us about all the other inhabitants of Dartmoor, the birds and insects, snakes and rodents, till the moor seems as busy and complicated as the greatest human city.

For readers of eleven upwards.

*Cover design by David Carl Forbes*

EWAN CLARKSON

# BREAK FOR FREEDOM

## The Story of a Mink

*Drawings by David Carl Forbes*

PENGUIN BOOKS

Penguin Books Ltd, Harmondsworth, Middlesex, England
Penguin Books Australia Ltd, Ringwood, Victoria, Australia

—

First published by Newnes 1967
Published in Puffin Books 1971

—



—

Made and printed in Great Britain
by Cox & Wyman Ltd, London,
Reading and Fakenham
Set in Intertype Baskerville

To Jenny – who cares

# Contents

# 1 Release

THE orange square of light in the house went out, and then there was only the moonlight, fitful and cloud-veiled, silvering the feathery tops of the pines, and etching strange profiles on the short, tussocky grass. The sheds lay in their oblongs of shadow, each housing a hundred mink, each open to the four winds, but offering some measure of protection from the glare of the sun, and the death-striking chill of the soft rain.

The mink were restless. Throughout the sultry heat of the September day they had lain sprawled on the wire floors of their pens, reluctant to feed, and waking only to bury their heads in the tepid water of their drinking bowls. With the coming of dark the temperature had dropped but a little, for there was no dew and the breeze, such as it was, blew light and warm.

Each mink lived from birth to death in a cage made from hexagonal-mesh wire, thirty-six inches long, eighteen inches wide, and a foot high. Each cage held an aluminium drinking bowl, wired to the mesh so that it could not be removed, and each had an opening at one end, which allowed access to the sleeping quarters, a wooden box five inches square and seven inches high. Even the floor of the sleeping box was of wire, and so it was ensured that the mink would grow their precious pelts without any danger of staining. The wire floors also ensured that the mink did not get wet, and so contract a sudden, fatal chill.

Some mink fed now, reaching up to the roof of the cage, where earlier in the evening the farmer had placed a spoonful of minced fish, liver, tripe, minced chicken heads, and cereal. Daintily the mink pulled the sloppy mess morsel by morsel through the wire. Any crumb that they did not eat immediately fell through the floor, so that there was no risk of an individual storing food in a corner of the cage, where it could go bad and later poison the animal's delicate digestive system.

Some of the mink groomed themselves, their lithe bodies twisting like eels as they nuzzled among the thick fur. Others ran ceaselessly back and forth, and here and there one played with its water pot, rattling it against the wire and spilling silver drops of water on to the ground below the cage. A few slept, curled in the narrow confines of their sleeping boxes. Except when they were asleep, the mink were rarely still for long, but occasionally one would cease its prowling or its play, to stand staring out through the mesh of the cage, peering with intense, myopic curiosity over the field, to where the guard fence, six feet high, and made of one-inch mesh, with a metal guard running the length of the top, isolated them from the English countryside.

Syla lived in one cage of a block she shared with forty-nine other females. At first glance she was identical with all the rest, about eighteen inches long, weighing some twenty-four ounces, and so dark brown in colour as to be almost black. Her face was wedge-shaped, her muzzle pointed, her ears small and rounded. Her eyes were dark and small, but sparkling bright, and her teeth sharp and white. Her feet were armed with tiny sharp claws, and were partially webbed, her body as lithe and stoat-like as the rest of the weasel tribe.

She was in the process of shedding her summer coat, and the first vestiges of the beauty that was to be her prime pelt were just beginning to show. Her tail was beginning to fill out, and from the thick under fur the guard hairs, each with its glossy sheen, projected to lie slightly at an angle to the body. Beneath her chin was a tiny white spot. She was exactly four months old.

Apart from the spot, she was identical with the others of her tribe, and similarly, apart from one tiny defect, her cage was identical with the others. The floor of her sleeping box was held with four staples, exactly like the rest, but here one staple had gone sideways into the wood so that the points protruded slightly into the box. This had passed unnoticed by the farmer, but Syla had discovered it many weeks ago, and at frequent intervals she chewed and scratched at the projection for no other reason than because it was there. Eventually, the staple dropped out, and now the wire had begun to sag slightly.

Many times of late she had thrust her nose at the yielding corner of wire. Always, when she drew back her head, the wire had sprung back into position. Tonight, when as usual she thrust against it, another staple gave up the unequal struggle, and suddenly, almost before she was aware of it, the floor dropped, and Syla lay bewildered on the ground.

Her first reaction was fear, and with the agoraphobia of her kind she moved quickly into the darkness beneath the shed, moving uncertainly among the sawdust, and the accumulated piles of ordure and waste food. A giant male mink screeched at her from the floor of his cage above, and she shied away, moving still further from the familiarity of her cage. Ahead of her lay the end of the shed, and the open field.

Her uneasy progress was seen and heard, in intimate detail, by a barn owl which sat on the peak of the shed roof. The owl knew about mink. Each night he came to perch on the shed roof, to wait for the voles that bred in great profusion among the coarse grasses of the field, and which came to scavenge among the food scraps below the pens. It was easy hunting. He waited until the vole was within range, and then lofted from his perch, closed his wings, and dropped. His talons would close, and he would pause, wings outstretched, huddling on the ground, until the absence of movement from the furry being in the grip of his claws drained away the last vestiges of the almost orgiastic ecstasy he had experienced in the kill. Then he would return to the roof, transfer the vole to his beak, and gulp it down.

Now he sat cautiously, peering down at Syla quartering the ground below him. He had examined the mink in the cages, and having satisfied himself they could do him no harm, he had ignored them. This was the first time he had seen one out of a cage, and he felt uneasy. He knew he was safe on the roof; his anxiety stemmed from more practical motives. Some weeks ago a doe rat had burrowed under the high wire guard fence, and led her family of young to the rich feeding beneath the mink pens. Now the young rats came alone, for their mother had abandoned them, and was already nursing a fresh brood of naked pink babies. Each night the barn owl took one of the elder brood, until now there was but a sole survivor, even now feeding just out of range. Syla was just six feet away from the rat, and drawing nearer. The barn owl waited, and watched from wide, unblinking eyes.

To Syla, the first whiff of scent from the rat, pungent, musky, hot-blooded, brought a feeling of intense, intoxicating excitement. She trembled violently, so that her jaw chattered, and saliva ran in thin streams among the roots of her teeth. She stood motionless, poised like a statue in the poor light, straining to locate the direction of the scent. Suddenly she darted to the left, paused a moment, and crossed to the right, as age-old hunting instincts came to her aid. Now she had pinpointed the whereabouts of her prey, but the movements had alerted the rat and he stood motionless, ready to flee. Syla was within a yard of him, and moving in for the kill, almost mad with excitement, when he bolted.

Syla followed, and the young rat led her along a barely perceptible furrow, straight through the hole in the fence.

The rat led her through thick undergrowth of bramble and bracken, into a gap in a dry stone wall, and out on to a mossy garden path. Syla, cage-bound, and unfamiliar with the terrain, was rapidly losing ground, but she followed doggedly on through a hedge of holly and hawthorn, down into a small, disused quarry. Here the rat went to ground, lost amid a confusion of scents that baffled Syla and reduced her to exhausting, chittering rage.

The barn owl remained motionless on the mink shed roof. The clouds had gone now, and the moon shadows lengthened with the dying night. Another hour passed, and the world grew darker. There was a slight movement in the grass, but the owl did not stir. Another movement, and a black shape detached itself from the shed roof to drop silently into the shadows. It wanted an hour before the dawn, and the thin shriek of the dying vole echoed and re-echoed throughout the meadows and woodlands of England, as it had done each night since long before the first tramp of the Roman Legions.

The cry was repeated in the quarry, as Syla came unexpectedly on a young bank vole, asleep in a nest of carefully shredded paper and rags under an old tea chest. Syla's teeth bit into the skull of the vole without any premeditation, and for the first time in her life she knew the fierce, satisfying joy of the predator. Then she ate the head, the heart, and the liver of the vole, before curling up in the tea chest to sleep.

Dawn came, and with the first light the trees and plants, grasses and ferns, shrubs and hedgerows ceased to absorb oxygen, and began to convert the carbon dioxide into starch, charging the air instead with the life-giving oxygen without which no animal could live. The owl drifted away to the barn where in silent meditation and half slumber he passed the day, and one by one the bats returned to their holes under the thatch. The otter slept where dawn overtook him, curled among the ferns by the river, and the cattle in the meadow stirred, beginning slowly to drift over to the gate near the milking parlour. Blackbirds chinked from the hedgerows, and a robin sang his September territorial song. The day was beginning, a day in which many of the population of the wild were yet to be born, and in which many were to die. Already the sun was warm, and once again it promised to be sultry.

# 2 The Tip

THE quarry where Syla slept had been disused since shortly after the farm had been built. Water seeped through faults in the granite of the cliff face, moistening the rock and nourishing the mosses and ferns that grew there. Scrub oak overhung the dell, shading the floor from the summer sun, and each autumn carpeted the rock-strewn floor with leaves, which rotted down into a sour, acid humus. Here and there tall spindly shrubs had sprung up, saplings of ash and sycamore, clumps of alder and hazel, thrusting upwards in search of the light.

Parasites clung around them. Twining tendrils of honeysuckle intermingled with thick twisting stems of ivy, so that here and there the poor thin trees had broken under the strain of the extra weight, and slumped to the quarry floor to rot and decay. In the spring, while there was still light, primroses shone their pale stars, followed later by wild hyacinths, which flowered in the dappled light of May, screened by the young leaves of the trees, yet still able to draw their strength from the sun. Then the bracken grew, and the questing, searching finger tips of the brambles, and only the fireweed could find strength to rise above the smothering carpet of growth. In one corner, a badger had his sett, and here the ground elder flourished, but elsewhere nothing could compete with the bracken. Only the bramble could climb above it.

Other trees grew, holly and elder, with their clusters of berries, attracting the birds, and at the edge of the quarry was a grove of broom. This had been sown by wood ants, who had brought the oil-bearing seed over a great distance. Most of the seeds had been destroyed, but here and there some accident had befallen the laborious little porter, causing her to abandon her load, and so the seed had taken root.

The quarry teemed with life. Lizards lived high up on the cliff, and in the summer every bush and shrub that clung to the rock was alive with tiny young, basking in the sunlight and feeding on the minute insects that congregated on the leaves. Amongst the rotting wood lived slow worms, and in the moister parts of the dell were frogs and toads. Voles, mice, and rats abounded, squabbling at night when the glow worms lit the under sides of the leaves.

Birds came all the time; in the spring to nest, in summer to feed on the insect life, in autumn for the berries, and in winter for the shelter from the icy wind. A nuthatch had a nest each year in the biggest holly tree, in a hole where a branch had broken away, and throughout the year his tapping could be heard, at all hours of the day, like a tiny hammer, as he searched for grubs among the rotting bark of the trees. Sometimes a wood owl came to pass the hours of daylight, but always the smaller birds found him, and gave him no peace until they had driven him away.

The family at the farm used the quarry as a tip, and for generations all the household rubbish had been dumped here. As each successive generation grew more affluent, so the amount and quality of the rubbish increased. Worm-eaten wood was mixed with rolls of old wire netting. Tin cans were legion, some rusted away, some new and shiny, lying half filled with rain water. In each tiny reservoir mosquito larvae had hatched, hanging head down in the stagnant water, their feathery breathing-plumes just touching the surface.

Wooden boxes, rags, old kettles and oildrums littered the floor of the quarry. Grotesquely, a doll's head lay smashed in, and separated from its body, and a thick book lay half open, as if dropped by a careless or startled reader.

Several times during the day Syla woke and stirrred, but she was stiff from her unaccustomed exertion of the previous night, and her feet, which all her life had been accustomed to the feel of wire netting, were raw and painful from contact with the hard ground. Once she crept out from the ruined tea chest, to lap water from one of the cans, but it was stale and distasteful to her palate, used only to fresh tap water constantly renewed, and after slaking her thirst she returned to her hideout, and lay looking out into the westering sun.

Towards evening Rust came down to the quarry to hunt. Rust was the biggest and oldest of the farm cats, a martyr throughout his life to a chronic ear disease. Soon after he was born, small silver-grey parasites migrated from the ears of his mother and took up residence in his. Here they lived and loved, mated and died, fluctuating in numbers, but ever present to lay their eggs and creep about on the cartilages of his ears, so that never in his life had he known relief from their irritation. His two brothers and his sister, one of which was black and the other two dark tabby, all carried the same parasite, without suffering in the slightest. Rust was different, and at first he tried in vain to relieve the irritation by raking with his strong back claws, tearing great lumps of pale sandy fur from around his neck and head. Gradually he so bruised and damaged the lining of his ears that they became distorted, and from time to time they turned septic, and ran with a yellow discharge. Occasionally someone would remark on the state of his ears, but no one did anything, and now they were occluded with small, cauliflower-shaped growths. Rust was stone deaf, but his sight was keen.

Rust knew about the vole in the tea chest, for he had spent a long time waiting for it the afternoon before. He did not know that the vole had died suddenly in the night, or that the tea chest had a new lodger. He lay down about a foot from the hole in the side of the box, curled his paws delicately beneath his chest, and waited, one tattered ear twitching slightly.

Syla crouched in the darkest corner of the tea chest, trembling with apprehension at the arrival of the stranger. Rust half slept, his eyes open, confident that the slightest scent of the stirring vole, or the smallest flicker of movement would prod him into alertness. Time passed. The red sun sank below the skyline, and dark caverns began to grow among the oaks. Blackbirds began to chink sleepily in the bushes high on the cliffs, and a woodpigeon flew in fast and low, to pitch noisily in the branches of the oak, where it settled to roost.

With the coming of darkness Syla's courage began to grow. Her first unreasoning terror at the sight of Rust left her, her fur, which had stood fluffed out on end, making her look twice her normal size, once more laid down flat, and she made small hesitant moves towards the hole outside which Rust lay. Each time, at the sight of the cat, her nerve failed her, and so, realizing that her exit was barred, she began to explore each corner of the chest. At one point she discovered a thin current of cooler air, and towards this she began to dig, tearing aside the litter of cloth and paper without any difficulty. As she burrowed down, the current of air grew stronger, until at last she discovered a hole, barely two inches in diameter, but quite large enough for her to slip through. Rust, his deaf ears conveying no clue of this activity, waited on, as the moon rose higher and higher in the sky, and the dew settled thick and white across the fields.

By this time Syla was three fields away, leaping through the long grass which soaked her chest and thighs. It was an enjoyable feeling for her, to feel fresh moisture for the first time, flattening her fur, weighting it down, and wrapping it in close embrace around her limbs. She had forgotten completely about the mink farm. That part of her life had been wiped out with the traumatic experience within the tea chest, and her deliberate escape had destroyed the previous feeling of security that such objects had hitherto engendered. In abandoning the tea chest and the tip she had cast off the last of the shackles that linked her to mankind. She did not realize it, but she was free. She only knew that it was a fine thing to run in the moonlight, breasting the waves of grass and plunging her face into the cold dew.

Her exuberance gradually became tempered with hunger, and as she slipped through the hedge and into the next field she began to quarter the ground in search of prey. She stayed close to the hedge mound, for here the scents were thickest, and the grass was cropped short. Lobworms lay stretched on the turf, their tiny cilia rasping on the grass as they lay groping blindly, their strong, prehensile tails locked fast in the mouth of the burrows from which they had emerged, their ringed bodies glistening in the moonlight. Each worm sought the company of another, hermaphrodite like itself, for even worms may experience moments of ecstasy.

Syla sniffed cautiously at the first of the worms, and was mightily astonished when the worm drew suddenly back into its burrow. She snapped at the head, removing the tip of the prostomium, and chewed it, relishing the strange, earthy flavour. The second worm she grabbed more adroitly, crushing down on it as it writhed in her jaws. This she ate, and then three more, before finding the diet oddly nauseating and unsatisfying, while the slime clung to her cheeks, offending her sense of the fastidious.

She wandered on, and a frog, itself engrossed in a diet of earthworms, leapt in front of her. Syla pounced, and ate the hindlegs, before stuffing the still palpitating corpse into a mousehole in the hedge bank. The mink sought another taste of the fresh, warm blood she had experienced for the first time the previous night, and she was tantalized by the strong odours of voles that were all around her.

She moved up on to the top of the hedge mound, following the worn pathways that twisted and wound among the gnarled roots of hawthorn, blackthorn and beech, until at last her way was barred by the rotten stump of a great ash tree. The tree was buried beneath a thick growth of ivy, which effectually thatched the top of the stump, and concealed the many entrances to its hollow interior. Here the scent of vole was very strong, and Syla quested about, climbing like a cat among the thick ivy stems, until at last she came upon an opening. She slid inside, and crawled into the upper, smaller hollow of the stump, and here a female vole ran shrieking from her nest, leaving her litter of naked pink young sprawled in blind abandon on the short dry grass. Syla ate all six, and fell asleep almost immediately.

# 3 The Hedgerow

THE hedgerow was very old, laid down at the time when Norman warriors were invading English shores. The mound on which it grew was wide and high, covering many acres of good arable ground, but it afforded shelter to the sheep that were brought down from the moor in winter, and broke the dry winds of March, that threatened to sweep away the light top soil that was exposed after ploughing.

Many species of shrub grew there, hawthorn and beech, holly and elder, blackthorn, hazel, spindleberry and rowan, with here and there great thickets of gorse. Slow of growth in the well-drained soil of the mound, combed and shaped by the prevailing wind, twisted and gnarled by the attentions of the hedger, the hedge acted as host to many underlings. Honeysuckle, its petals frayed by the destructive dormice, climbed up the hawthorn to seek the light. Other climbers, too, clung and clawed, struggled and wove their way upwards. The bryony embraced the beech, and the ivy clung to the hawthorn. Old man's beard spread its feathery plumes, and intertwined among all were the vetches. On the mound primroses grew, then, each in its season, came the violets, the wild hyacinths, the campions, the foxgloves, the meadowsweet, and the ferns. Each plant had its own requirements as to shade and moisture. Each flourished as conditions became right.

The hedge was food and shelter to a host of small creatures. Thrushes nested in the thickets, and sought the snails that lived on the mound, taking those which, because of their coloration, least matched the colour of their surroundings. These they destroyed, breaking the snails on small flat stones, and so the thrushes helped the snails to survive, thinning out the ones less suited to survival, and leaving room for others, better camouflaged.

All life in the hedge, each separate individual species, was interdependent on the other. The fate of one had a marked influence on the rest. Once the hedge had abounded with rabbits, preserved by the landowner for the meat and sport they provided. Their burrows riddled the hedge mound, draining it and drying it so that only a bare covering of vegetation grew there. Clover grew in the field, and the rabbits fed well on the protein-rich leaves, but still the clover grew.

Then came a plague, a virus which was injected into the bloodstream of the rabbit by the sting of a mosquito, or the bite of a flea. Crowded together in the mound, the rabbits spread the disease quickly amongst themselves, and one by one they staggered blindly about the fields, their bodies swollen and distorted, finally to die in strange and contorted attitudes. The crows and the buzzards flocked to the feast, and then it was over, except for a few individual rabbits which had survived the plague, and which began to create a new colony.

The predators, the hawks and the owls, weasel, stoat, fox and badger, polecat, marten, otter, and the lean domestic cats which roamed wild in the woods, turned from the young rabbit to the vole, and soon the voles which had swarmed on the acres of arable land, were reduced to a tenth of their previous numbers. Starving, the predators did not breed, and so the voles were able to breed unmolested. Mature in five weeks, giving birth three weeks later, one female in a year could repopulate a field.

The voles ate vegetable matter, but they also ate insects, and they sought out the nests of the bumble bees, destroying the grubs. So there were no bumble bees to fertilize the clover, and so the patch that had supported the rabbits for so long began to dwindle and fade.

Syla stayed in the ash stump for many days, learning to hunt, to select her prey and to kill efficiently. She had, at first, been lucky, and she was soon to discover that it was not always so easy to catch her prey. Often she went hungry, but always she managed to make a meal of sorts, and always there was the ash stump for shelter.

It was autumn, the time of the fat, and the hedge sagged under the weight of its fruit and berries. Countless millions of spiders spread their webs over the dew-drenched stubble, traps for the teeming hosts of gnats that hovered in the still warm air. Birds fed on the berries of hawthorn and holly, spreading the seeds far and wide. Throughout the long, mild nights Toschick the hedgehog ate and ate and ate, piling on layers of fat that would nourish him through the winter.

Brock ate well too, foraging along the hedgemound. He sought big lobworms, a wasp's nest, a cluster of baby voles, snails, bluebell bulbs, a lizard, cockchafer grubs. Any food that his keen nose could find, that his powerful claws could unearth, was eaten with noisy appreciation. Once he found half a pork pie left by a child picking blackberries, and every night after that for a week he checked the spot, to see if his good fortune would be repeated.

The stubble fields were rich in fallen grain, and here came rooks in noisy conclaves, grey ghost flocks of wood-pigeons, and small groups of birds, gaudy of plumage, long of tail, with spurs on their legs. Few farmers could afford to rear pheasants these days, but the owner of the land was rich, and still managed to spend a few thousand pounds on his shooting.

The eggs had been bought from a game farm many miles away, hatched in an incubator, and hand reared on specially purchased food. Next they had been transferred to folds, and distributed about the farm in carefully chosen localities. Then they were gradually allowed their freedom, while the gamekeeper kept a close watch for the unwelcome attentions of a marauding fox or hawk, stoat or brown rat.

One evening in late September, before the sun had set, Syla slipped out of the hollow in the ash. She was hungry, although she had fed well the night before, and she had a strange craving which, although she did not attempt to understand, or define it, nagged her and made her feel ill at ease. She had been restless all day, and when she had slept she had dreamt of the night when she had played with the dew. Syla needed water, and a change of diet. She was missing her fish.

The sun was dying, staining the sky in the west to deep crimson. The sunlight was reflected in the rose glow of the stubble fields, and the shoulder of the sleeping hill wore a cloak of burnished copper. Autumn smouldered like a torch, ready to flame at the touch of the frost, and as the light faded the mist towered like smoke over the serried ranks of the oaks. Syla moved quickly and jerkily along the top of the hedge-mound, blind to the beauty of the evening, but alive to the smells and sounds of the awakening night. She heard the melancholy call of Ronk the crow, as he winged slowly towards the wood, and marked the rustle of a grass snake as it slid out of her way. The shadows were lengthening now, and the first stars of evening were beginning to glow, pale and yellow, in the indigo sky. Syla heard a sudden heavy plop, and froze as a large shape loomed in the hedge ahead.

The hen pheasant shook her feathers, which had been ruffled by the exertion of climbing the mound, and looked about her for a suitable perch. A holly grew here, its grey scaly trunk leaning at a crazy angle. It divided at a broad notch, where once the hedger's hook had laid it low, and above this the bush spread out into a warm thicket of prickly leaves. The pheasant flew up into the notch and sank down to roost, outlined black against the sky.

Stealthily, Syla followed, her sharp claws gripping the bark of the holly and supporting her light weight so that she climbed as nimbly as a cat. She covered the last foot in a sudden rush, sinking her teeth into the bird's wing as the pheasant woke to sudden panic. There was a violent squawking, a crashing in the leaves, and pheasant and mink fell out of the hedge and into the field.

The pheasant thrashed helplessly, striking with its beak and kicking out at the vicious little animal that clung so doggedly, and who bit so cruelly that already the bones of the wing were crushing under the strain. Suddenly Syla released her grip, only to renew it an inch nearer the bird's neck. She was oblivious to the buffeting the pheasant was giving her, and the more she was flung about, the tighter she clung on, her eyes closed in grim ecstasy, her forepaws tucked safely out of the way, and her hindlegs ready to kick and rip whenever the opportunity presented itself. Gradually the bird's struggles grew weaker, until at last it lay like a wrecked galleon, its beak agape, its fading life a red mist in its eyes, so that as the teeth of the mink closed on the neck of the bird in the final bite, death came almost as a caress.

Syla ate little of the pheasant. She took the brain, and drank the blood, then after worrying at the neck and strewing feathers over the grass, she left it. Before she went, however, she did a strange thing. Carefully, she climbed on top of the body, her tail raised, and carefully anointed the carcase with musk from the gland at the base of her tail. So, later in the night, when a fox came upon the corpse, he passed by in mingled fear and disgust.

Next morning, when the mist cleared, Ronk and his mate found the pheasant. For an hour they sat huddled in the hedge three feet away, cawing softly to each other and stealing long, mournful glances at the corpse. Then, casually, Ronk planed down to the field, strolled over to the pheasant, and, with the utmost delicacy, seized it by the tip of one wing and dragged it away from the spot where it had lain. Only then, when they were satisfied that there was no trap, did the two crows start to feed.

The farmer saw them from three fields away, and went quietly for his gun, but long before he got within range of the birds they heard him, and flew away, cawing derisively. The farmer lingered for a few moments, bending thoughtfully over the bird before returning to his work, and leaving the pheasant where it lay. In the afternoon the crows returned, and they had almost finished with the carcase when they felt the first knife pains of the strychnine that the farmer had laid in the bird. He found them both later, and for many weeks they hung together, head downward, turning slowly in the wind.

After killing the pheasant, Syla continued to follow the hedge. She had no interest in hunting or food, and as the moon rose higher and higher in the sky, she journeyed on, following the intricate highways of the hedges, crossing field after field, always, perhaps unconsciously, perhaps obeying some primitive instinct, perhaps because the shape of her body made it easier for her, for some reason, journeying steadily downhill.

She came at last to a small wood on a hill, where stunted oaks grew out of a clitter of great moss-rotten granite boulders. The oaks had survived because of the boulders, for the acorns had long ago fallen into the cracks and crevices between the stones, and here had found moisture, shade, and a little nourishment on which to grow. So the acorns had put down roots, and the boulders had protected the young trees from frost and grazing animals, while the roots, bound firm under the rocks had held the trees safe against the force of the strongest winds. Starved, stunted, twisted and gnarled beyond all resemblance of trees, yet the oaks had survived, and had grown harder and tougher than their giant relatives. Some of them were over three hundred years old.

Dawn was breaking, and the mist showed grey. Syla climbed wearily on to the knotted bole of a tree and crawled out on to a branch. Here in a fork, where a mass of debris, twigs, moss and leaves had gathered to form a platform, on which grew ferns and blueberries, Syla curled up and went to sleep. The sun warmed her, and the faint breeze made the airy platform sway gently to and fro, lulling her even deeper into sleep. She did not hear the rattle of shotguns echoing from the farm she had just left. It was the first of October, and pheasant shooting had begun.

# 4 The Hill Stream

MANY pairs of eyes watched Syla as she slept. Torag the buzzard, wheeling high over the wooded hill, marked her as she rocked in her airy bed, and dropped down lower to survey the strange object. Torag led a strange double existence, a life spent partly in the air, and devoted to lofty aerial ballet, dancing great wheeling circles in the clouds, as the sunset stained the sky yellow and highlighted the gold of his plumage; and partly on the ground, where he was big and clumsy, gawky and scared, a shifty-eyed scavenger and eater of carrion.

Torag perched uneasily on a high oak branch and watched the mink. Syla breathed gently and evenly, and soon the faint movement of her breathing became apparent to the buzzard, who flapped heavily away and began to quarter the marsh beyond the woodland, looking for frogs and beetles. Torag was not proud, and he had a large appetite.

Then came Thalos and his wandering band. There were nine of them altogether, himself and his mate, with seven grown-up youngsters, survivors of a clutch of eleven which the long-tailed tits had raised in a tall domed nest of feathers and moss. Together they roamed the woodlands and hedgerows, never lingering more than a few minutes in one place, never spreading very far apart, continually calling to each other as they sought their diet of spiders, grubs and insects. They perched in a twittering group in the oak above Syla, surveying her from all angles, and enjoying a delicious thrill from the nearness of this strange predator. Syla shivered in her sleep and the flock trooped away, further into the wood. In a few minutes they had forgotten all about her.

The weather was changing. The light breeze was freshening, turning the yellowing leaves of the oaks and sending dark feathery clouds scudding across the face of the sun. A few spots of rain fell, cold and stinging, enough to sharpen the acid smell of autumn, and to wake Syla from her sleep. A cock pheasant crowed his survival of the day's shooting, and overhead a huddle of rooks and jackdaws clamoured as they hurried homeward.

Syla climbed down the oak and began to make her way along the base of the hill, still keeping inside the wood, picking her way round the clitter of stones and boulders. The going was rough. Brambles trailed their spiky fingers over the sour ground, and crumbling mats of rotten twigs and leaves hid gaps and crevices among the rocks. Gradually the stones grew less frequent, and the bramble gave way to heather and wortleberry, which in turn led Syla to the marsh. Here mosses and lichens grew in a quaking mat over the waterlogged peat, and the sundew spread its sticky petals to trap the flies that bred there.

Syla pattered over the moss until she came to a clear pool, which overspilled and drained away down hill. She followed the tiny watercourse, as yet a mere stain on the hillside, quickening her speed as the stain became a gutter, and the gutter a swiftly flowing drain. Now the music of the rushing water was loud in her ears, and the sweet sour smell of the moss was strong in her nostrils, so she hastened on, coming at last to a tiny fall, where a lone hawthorn bush grew, and a clear pool among the rocks reflected the image of the tree.

Syla buried her nose and drank deep. Then she slid luxuriously into the cold, clear water and swam across to the other side, pattering out among the stones and shaking silver drops from her fur. Immediately she turned and re-entered the water, diving and somersaulting, picking pebbles from the bed of the pool and holding them in her paws, dropping them, and diving to retrieve them before they reached the bottom. She had never swum in her life before, and yet she was more at home in the water than she was on land.

At length she ceased her play and continued her journey down river, sometimes following the bank, sometimes swimming downstream. At times the water was not deep enough to cover her, and nowhere was it more than a foot wide. The coarse reeds and grasses overhung the banks, and the heather and the gorse grew together to obscure the course of the stream, but here and there Syla found other pools, and gradually the size of the stream was swelling.

In one of the pools Syla saw the silvery gleam of her first trout, as the little fish fled from her approach. The mink hastened in pursuit, but the fish had gone, down through the shallows into the swift stickle below. Syla lingered on, rooting under the banks, and turning over the smaller of the flat stones on the river bed, until she was rewarded by the glimpse of a flat writhing tail. Feverishly she scrabbled with her claws, and seeing another glimpse of a shining body she bit deep, seizing the eel and dragging it to the surface. Triumphantly she bore her prey to the bank and ate it ravenously, crunching through the tiny bones and savouring the rich, curdy flesh.

By now it was raining steadily, and it had grown quite dark. Dark clouds obscured the light of the moon, but Syla found two more eels, and a loach, by the same process of turning over stones. The trout continued to elude her, and now the weight of the rain began to make itself felt. For hours it had fallen, silver drops clinging to every leaf and twig, every stone, every grass blade, every frond of fern. Slowly the raindrops trickled down to the ground, swelling the soil, draining downwards, filling the great sponge of the peat. Soon the peat began to overflow, and the acid brown water filled the little stream. Long before dawn Syla was forced to retreat, to make her way overland, past snorting panicking sheep, in search of warmth and shelter.

She felt strangely unwell, shivering with cold, and exhausted with the weight of water in her long thick fur. She came at last to a dry stone wall, and worked her way along, seeking a gap that might lead to a shelter. Finding one, she wormed her way inside, wearily rubbing herself against the stone, and wringing out some of the excess moisture. The wall was a labyrinth of galleries and passages, strongly smelling, reeking with the must of resident voles and shrews, grass snakes, adders, stoats and weasels. Here and there were collections of dry fern and moss, the remains of long disused nests, and these Syla used to dry herself. Gradually, warmth returned to her, and her strength returned as she shed her load of moisture.

Wrens fluttered away in front of her, chittering angrily as she drove them out into the night. A hunting stoat paused on the scent of a vole, and stared inquiringly as Syla bustled towards him. He felt no enmity or anger, only a mild curiosity, but Syla, her nerves strained with tiredness and the excitement of the night, screamed hysterically and showed her teeth. The stoat was reminded of the behaviour of his mate, who earlier in the year had warned him away from her kitts, and so he stepped prudently aside, anxious to avoid an argument with a neurotic female.

At last Syla found a space between two large stones, deep enough and wide enough for her to curl round in, and at least dry and airy.

She slept fitfully, shivering violently, and bordering on a chill that could easily have led to a serious lung congestion, had she not been meticulous in drying herself before settling to rest. Her feed of eels rested uneasily in her stomach, for although her system demanded fish, she had of late grown unaccustomed to it. Indeed, she had fed very badly since her escape from the farm. She had lost a considerable amount of weight, and only her surplus fat had kept her going while she learnt the rudiments of hunting. In many ways she had been fortunate. She had escaped just when food was most plentiful, and her early days of freedom had been favoured with fine weather. Just in time she had found the stream which could supply her with fish, but winter was fast approaching, and she had a lot still to learn.

Syla emerged from the wall while it was still light, and made her way immediately towards the stream. The rain had ceased, but grey clouds still hung over the landscape, and a soft, warm mist was rising from the sodden meadows. The river was unfishable, swirling by in a swollen brown flood, obliterating the pools and hiding the eels and trout that Syla craved. She turned instead to the meadows, finding small frogs, sweet and succulent, unlike the large one she had found some time ago. Then she caught a vole, pouncing in a most professional manner as the tiny mammal ventured out from the shelter of a gorse bush.

The hill farm through which the stream flowed was, unlike the previous one, poor and ill kept. The walls were ruinous and tumbling, the hedges overgrown, the ditches choked. Weeds, docks, thistles and straggly bracken grew in the boggy pastures, and moss clung to the rotten thatch of the barn. The lanes were rutted and sticky with mud, while most of the gates hung drunkenly on broken hinges, supported by whiskery lengths of binder twine and reinforced with hazel sticks cut from the hedges.

Many years ago the farmer, while still a young man, had come to the hill farm with his wife and baby, fired with ambition to create a model farm. Gradually the cold and damp combined to inflict his wife with arthritis, so that she could not help him in the fields, or with the milking, or the hens. As the son grew he saw the futility of the struggle, and watched his father grow older, and weaker, but no richer. The son hated the farm and the sour, slobbery ground, turning instead to the nearby town, and the security of employment mending farm machinery.

The farmer felt no bitterness, but gradually he relaxed the unequal struggle, content to watch the farm decay and deteriorate. He still kept a few cows and pigs, grew what roots he had time for, and lived as much as possible off the land. For pocket money he turned to the market, buying and selling with a frugality and shrewdness that showed him a small but regular profit, and which earned him a name locally as a reliable and honest dealer. He even derived a certain pleasure from watching the forces of the wild reclaim their own from the farm.

In her wanderings Syla came upon a ruinous shed, set in the corner of one of the fields, and almost hidden in a luxuriant growth of bramble, elder, and nettles. The granite walls were moss-rotten, crumbling, and bowed with the weight of ivy. Here and there tiles were missing from the roof, and the wormy beams sagged beneath the weight of the heavy red tiles. Through the years, rain and snow had driven in, rotting the upper floor, while the ground floor, which was of earth, was damp and foul with decaying remains of root crops, hay, and straw. There was no door.

Syla ventured in, and immediately there was a frenzied squeaking and scurrying as a host of rats, of all ages and sizes scampered away into their holes in the floor. Syla, her nose and whiskers twitching, followed, voicing her excitement in a high-pitched buzz. High above her, in the cobwebby shadows of the rafters, the bats were engrossed in an orgy of promiscuous love making, for it was autumn, and the time for their mating. They ignored Syla. Indeed, it is doubtful whether they were aware of her presence. For the rats there began a night of frenzy and terror, as during the long hours of darkness, up and down the galleries which undermined the floor, they were hunted without mercy by this stranger, this wicked little hunter with the merciless jaws and the relentless persistence of her kind.

Rats died, their throats torn, left to bleed in the darkness. Rats met Syla face to face in the narrow tunnels, and were slain as they attempted to turn and flee. Rats were cornered in the nurseries where they had been born, and where they had reared their own families. Syla killed and killed, chopping and slashing in a paroxysm of blood lust, as each fresh victim screamed with fear at the sight of her. Long before dawn the rats which had survived streamed out of the shed in a brown flood, seeking the sanctuary of the overgrown hedges and dry stone walls, never to return to their former home.

Syla stayed on in the shed, sleeping among a heap of straw and hay, long abandoned, but still dry and free from mould. The first frosts came, silvering the meadows and crushing the red bracken so that it crumbled to the ground, singeing the tips of the grasses, and bringing the yellow and gold leaves fluttering from the oaks. Syla lingered on, undisturbed in the shed, and left alone to practise her trout fishing. She learnt to slip silently, without splash, into the foot of a pool, swimming up behind the trout as they lay with heads upstream. Before she could quite reach them they would dart away, up to the head of the pool, but here they would turn, to come darting downstream again, and Syla learned to mark her victim down, to station herself in anticipation of its return flight, and to meet it with open jaws and grasping, needle claws.

# 5 The River

THE land was ablaze with the cold fires of autumn, and gradually, as the great weight of vegetation withered and died, as the plant roots gave up the struggle to absorb moisture from the soil, and the green stems shrivelled and turned brown, as the leaves detached themselves one by one from countless thousands of twigs, so, through the mists that hung in the clear cold air, the naked land exposed its bareness to the cleansing of the rain and the cold. New beauty became apparent. New scenes opened up through the bare hedgerows; hills, gently curving, stretched away into the far distance, lost in a purple haze, and on the moor great grey rocks lay crouched like patient beasts, sleeping on a fox-red quilt of bracken. Now the real beauty of the oaks was revealed, as the delicate tracery of twigs was etched sharply against a sky, now dove-grey, now saffron-yellow, now indigo in the long twilight.

The visitors had gone, after many days spent in anxious conclave on the telephone wires beside the road. The swallows and the martins always seemed reluctant to depart, but others seemed to slip away, silently, in the night, without so much as a last look round. The yellow wagtail and the tree pipit, the flycatchers and the warblers, the blackcap and the white throat, all the life that had filled the lush vegetation with noise and movement had gone with the passing of September. The chiffchaff lingered on, high in the bare branches, as if undecided whether or not to leave.

At night, when the stars burned bright with frost fire, and the moon glowed with a whiteness that spoke of harder times to come, the skies were alive with travellers, as innumerable hordes of birds left the barren, cold land mass that was the continent, risking the arduous sea journey to seek the warmth of the wave-lapped island, and its moist, dank climate. Fieldfares came, great grey thrushes with guttural northern voices, and with them, the delicate redwings. Curlew whistled urgently overhead, and the wind whistled in the pinions of the wild grey geese. Others came too, long-eared and snowy owls, osprey, goshawk, rare individuals which did not pass unnoticed for long, and which, when they were spotted, were shot, because man feared anything that was strange.

The trout was spawning, cutting their redds in the clean gravel of the stream. Thus preoccupied, they became easy prey for Syla, and in the little dark days before the turn of the year Syla fed well, hunting and fishing mainly by day, for no human came to disturb her.

After the floods of autumn the weather had been dry, and for some time the stream had flowed shallow and clear. Syla's tracks were plain on every little mudbank and sandbar, and here and there, on the dry stones that bordered the stream, small traces, fish scales, bitten fins, and gill covers, showed where she had dined. Here and there, on an alder stump, a boulder, a tuft of dried grass, she left her droppings, like an otter's spraint, only smaller.

The water bailiff spotted the signs straight away, for he was a man long trained in such matters. He came seldom to the small stream, for the sea trout did not come up so far, and the little brown trout were not worthy of the angler's lure, or the poacher's snare. Once in a while, however, he walked by the stream, to satisfy himself that no danger threatened the river lower down, and to acquire some of the farmer's cider. Now he puzzled over the tracks and signs by the stream, but it was not until he was driving home in his car that he realized what they were. Then he remembered that there had been some reports that mink were escaping from captivity, and that some had even been known to breed in the wild. Mink farms had grown more numerous in the South West, ever since the farmers had discovered that the moist, warm climate had seemed to suit the fur. Now the government had made it an offence to keep mink without a licence, and those wishing to farm had to comply with strict regulations. Any mink seen running wild were to be shot, and it was also an offence to allow mink to exist on your land, without endeavouring to remove them.

The next day the bailiff returned, and with him in the car he had two traps, long thin rectangular tunnels of wire mesh, with a door at each end, and a spring loaded plate in the middle. Above the plate was a hook. When set, a piece of fish hung on the hook, and to reach it the animal had to stand on the plate. This released the spring, which snapped the doors shut, not harming the mink, but imprisoning it alive.

Carefully the bailiff set the traps, baiting each with a piece of sea trout, one he had found dead that morning. Then he left the stream, and went away down to the river, where the sea trout were spawning. The traps stood stark by the waterside, the metal gleaming dully in the pale sunlight. Pica the magpie was the first to investigate. He had watched the bailiff arrive, seen him walk slowly along the river, observed his every movement as he set the traps. Pica owed his life to this habit of not minding his own business. Every day, as he went about his business, whether it was robbing a bird's nest, picking sheep ticks from the woolly fleece of their host, or stealing hen food from the chicken run, whatever his affairs, be they innocent, laudable, or nefarious, Pica knew that he must ever be alert, lest his last impression of life was to be a view of the twin evil eye of a twelve bore. He knew that he could avoid this fate by keeping track of his enemies, the humans, for he had discovered that they were regular in their habits. Thus if the farmer was milking the cows, Pica could depend on half an hour's solitude in the chicken run.

The bailiff was not on Pica's schedule, so the magpie watched silently, huddled, apparently miserable and disinterested in the hedge. Only when the sound of the car engine died away in the distance did Pica come to life, like an animated rag doll, flying straight to the first of the traps, and hopping jauntily up to it. At first he was cautious, stalking warily round and clacking loudly, as if warning himself not to take any chances. He peered in through each of the open doors, but made no attempt to put his head inside. Then he attempted to reach the fish through the mesh, but his beak was not long enough. Finally, screwing up his courage, he perched gingerly on top of the cage, and shook the hook holding the bait. Still he could not reach the fish, and still nothing happened.

Pica stood baffled, then he tried again, reaching down and grasping the shank of the hook, raising it so that the fish was lifted to the top of the cage. So far, so good, but when he let go the hook to grab the fish, it dropped down out of his reach. Now Pica had the answer, and carefully inserted one scaly leg through the mesh. Solemnly he raised the hook again with his beak, grasped the shank with his foot, and started to worry at the fish. The magpie chuckled with satisfaction. He was not really hungry, and he certainly did not need the fish, but he had beaten his arch enemy, and found a way to harass him, so he was well content.

He had eaten perhaps a quarter of the bait, or, more accurately, shredded it and thrown it away, when the bait became detached from the hook, and fell on to the plate. There was a loud snap, both doors sprang shut, and Pica took wing in a violent panic, a fear that turned to sudden pain. He had forgotten about his leg, inside the trap. In his fright he had automatically spread his claws, his foot had caught in the mesh, and the weight of the cage as he took flight snapped the thin, brittle bones of his shank like matchsticks.

At first the magpie collapsed helpless on top of the trap, but at last he managed to free his leg, and flop clumsily away to the shelter of the wood. There he brooded for several days, only venturing to feed when he was certain the coast was clear, until gradually his leg healed. Ever after, however, it was twisted, useless, and Pica's ways grew more evil than ever.

The other trap lay untouched throughout the day. Nevus, a carrion crow, marked it as he flew over, and checked momentarily in his flight. Then, suspicious, he righted himself and hurried on. He was a son of Ronk, who had died of poisoning, and the sole survivor of a clutch of four. A wandering stoat paused at the entrance to the trap, sniffing the bait, but the stoat was not a carrion eater, and did not even recognize the fish as food, so he too, moved on, and the trap lay, its doors agape in the gathering dusk.

As the first yellow stars began to glow feebly, a rat came down to the stream to drink. He was an old buck, scarred with the marks of many a battle, and full of the cunning of his kind. Yet he was a country rat, and knew nothing of the ways of mankind. Foxes and badgers, stoats and weasels, hawks and owls, were all enemies that he recognized, and he knew the ways of terriers, and ferrets, with their dreadful, pale pink eyes. Of traps he was as innocent as the day he was born, and so, when he came upon the cage with its bait of fish, he sauntered unconcernedly inside, trod heavily on the trap, and, with the sound of the closing doors ringing in his ears, began greedily to eat the fish. Then, when every scrap of bait had been demolished, he turned to leave.

Syla was late abroad that night, and the scream of rage from the frustrated rat was the first sound to reach her ears. The screams continued, and Syla hurried along the banks of the stream, consumed with curiosity, and anxious to see what was causing such a din. From the cage the rat gibbered at her, and Syla screamed back, frightened and nervous, she knew not why. She watched for a while, puzzled over the behaviour of this rat which did not flee from her, then, suddenly losing interest in a situation which did not alter, she loped away to hunt for voles.

Towards dawn the rat ceased his screaming, and stopped tearing at the bars of the cage with bloodstained, broken teeth, lapsing into a whimpering coma, part exhaustion, part fear. Here, as a gentle rain swept across the meadows, and a grey light lit the distant hills, the water bailiff found him. Gently the rat, still in the trap, was lowered into the stream. Soon the water reached his lungs, and the rat was free from his pain, from his fear, and the close confines of the trap.

The bailiff went thoughtfully back to the car, taking his traps with him. He returned a short while later, carrying a twelve bore shot gun, and turning up his collar against the rain, which now came in silvery, driving gusts, he settled in the lee of the rock, beside the biggest pool on the stream, and waited. Arda the heron spotted him while the bird was still high in the sky, over a mile away, and, croaking dismally, the great fisher turned aside, cranking on slow vanes towards the estuary five miles away. Arda had a horror of mankind. Gula the dipper flew past, perched for a moment, dropped a curtsey, and was gone.

Ispi the kingfisher was next, a flash of ultramarine and red, piping his shrill cry as he flew upstream. Still the bailiff sat on, while the rain soaked through his clothes, and the river began slowly to rise. A sudden snort beside him made him start, and slowly turn his head. A ring of silly moon faces stared at him, patient, sad eyes, slobbering noses, strongly smelling of milk. The farmer kept a few bullocks, and they, curious at the antics of this stranger, had come to watch. Their stupid company was the last straw, and bad-temperedly, the bailiff scrambled to his feet.

On his way back to the car the bailiff paused at the shed, half hesitated, and then went inside. Syla, asleep on the straw, heard his approach, and now lay wakeful, listening, hidden from view. The bailiff stood his gun in the corner, took off his coat, and from the pocket of his jacket took out cigarettes and matches. The sputter and flare of the match panicked Syla and she moved, rustling loudly in the straw and showing herself for an instant. With an oath, the bailiff dropped matches and cigarettes, jumping for his gun. As Syla bolted outside, the bailiff followed, cocking the hammers of the twelve bore, and the first shot blew a chunk of rotten granite from the shed, the dust stinging Syla as she dived for cover.

Inside, the yellow flame of the match, dropped by the bailiff at the sight of Syla, licked at the pile of straw. Hungrily it grew, spitting and crackling as if in anger at the squalor and ugliness around it, growing and spreading, turning the inside of the shed into a living rose of flame. Just in time the bailiff realized what was happening, and sprang in to rescue his coat. For a moment he looked around in panic, trying desperately to think of some way of saving the shed. Already, however, the flames were groping along the rafters, and the bats were fluttering helplessly about, seeking a way of escape. Some perished, but the rest left through the gaping holes in the roof.

Realizing the futility of trying to quell the blaze, the bailiff shrugged, and, somewhat crestfallen, went off to find the farmer, and confess what he had done. To his relief the farmer roared with laughter, said that ' 'T'wur a foine job,' and invited him to a jug of cider.

In her fear Syla ran downstream, further than she had ever gone before. Not much further, however, for all the time she had lived in the shed, and fished the small stream, she had not explored more than a hundred yards further downstream than she had gone the first night. Had she done so, she would have discovered the bridge, and the union of the stream with the big river. Here, amid a tangle of grey-green rock, and divided by a small island, a mere rock on which grew a riven rowan tree, the chatter and babble of the stream was lost, silenced in wonder at the mighty roar of the river, as thousands of gallons of white water thundered downhill on its way to the sea. Syla went to ground in a hollow below the rowan, while the rain fell, the river rose in spate, and the two men got drunk on the cider.

# 6 The Woodland Pool

RAIN is the spawn of the west wind, and with it he ravishes the wide moors, so that the dark and brooding hills conceive, and give birth to the rivers. From a placenta of peat or chalk, limestone or gravel, through small streams that are its umbilical cords, the river takes its life and its character. It may be long or short, large or small, acid or alkaline, swift or slow. The country through which it flows shapes this character, moulding it, strengthening or weakening, and as the centuries tick by, second by second, the forces of erosion combine and work with the river, so that its song is ever changing, old as time, yet ever new.

Below the bridge the river foamed and chattered through a clitter of giant moss-rotten granite boulders, lost to view below a tangle of green rock. Long ago, as the ice age receded before the warmth of the sea currents, when the oak forests of England lay shrouded in mist, and the beaver built their dams across the Thames, as the great snow drifts melted from the moors, then the river flowed quietly through a flat, wide valley.

Wind blew, and rain fell, washing away the softer earth of the hills. The river carried the earth away, and with it, sharp silt, which in the grip of the rushing water became a keen cutting tool. Steadily the river cut down into the valley, and slowly it drifted sideways to the south, leaving along its north bank great terraces of sand and gravel, its south bank cutting further and further into the hill, so that the sides of the cleave grew steeper.

Still the wind and the rain worked on the hilltops, and the hard granite rock alone stood fast against the forces of erosion. Rain soaked into the rock, and the frost froze the water, expanding it and breaking the rock. The sun shone, and again minute flakes of rock, shattered by unequal expansion, fell from the tors. Gradually larger rocks, rounded by erosion, loosened from their hold in the disappearing earth, slipped and fell downhill. They collected in a giant, tightly wedged heap along the bed of the river, settling more firmly as the river sang on, and cut underneath them. Still singing, the river worked on, cutting and carving, polishing and rounding, with a force as inexorable as time.

Below the cleave the river was tamed by a great shelf of rock. Here it eddied and foamed, gouging down into the bowels of the earth, and then, finding no outlet that way, it circled round, until its probing fingers found the lowest point on the sill of rock. Eagerly the river poured forth once more, but its speed had been slowed, and it was forced to drop its scythe of gravel. So it made for itself a bed, on which it idled, drifting quietly along until once more the resistance of the rocks made it turn abruptly aside. Here the river gouged a deep wide pool, before the hill fell away and the river could thunder on once more, eager to meet its death in the sea.

During the month that followed, Syla was to learn every inch of the stretch of river between the bridge and the woodland pool. She explored every twist and turn, every rock and tree stump, every gravel bar and sandspit, hunting and fishing by day or by night. She slept whenever she felt like it, curling up in one of a dozen snug retreats, a shelf of rock, deep under ground, littered with dry leaves and grasses, an ash stump, once used by an otter, and long ago abandoned. Sometimes she slept in the open, among a clitter of stones which sheltered her from the wind, and reflected the warmth of the thin sun on to her thick winter pelt.

She fed well, for the woodlands that surrounded the pool were rich in small mammals, mice and voles, squirrels, dormice, rats and shrews. Small birds, wrens, robins, tits and treecreepers haunted the dead undergrowth beneath the oaks. Syla grew sleek and round, laying on fat against the cold to come, and each day she swam in the cold acid waters of the river, hunting the trout which lay on the golden gravel.

Here man was an intruder, and the bare paths which led along the banks of the river had been pounded out by the feet of a tribe of badgers, whose setts honeycombed the side of the hill above the wood. The badgers had been there since Cromwell had fought his battles on the heath in the valley below, and countless generations lay entombed, sealed off in the passages in which they had died. Occasionally a badger, digging out a fresh tunnel, would come across the bones of one of his ancestors, and the bones would be pushed out of the sett with the soil, to lie bleaching in the sun which, years ago, had helped to form them.

Occasionally a lone badger would dig a sett away from the main fortress. A young sow, fearful, and anxious for solitude as the time for her confinement drew near; an old bachelor, bad tempered and crotchety with the aching of his teeth, and the rheumatism of his old bones. Sometimes setts were started, and then abandoned, after much labour, for one reason or another. Syla found such a sett, one morning when the air hung still, and moisture dripped from the bare branches of the oaks.

On a hot summer night, when Europe lay in darkness, and German bombs fell on English soil, a badger worked on his own fruitless errand of execution. In a hole close by the river a doe rabbit had a litter of young. The entrance to the burrow was wide and high, bigger in fact, than usual, and indeed a fox had scratched fruitlessly at the hole on several nights. The badger dug mightily, finding little resistance in the yielding soil, and so he enlarged the entrance, and dug his way along the burrow, where not more than five feet away the palpitating doe lay listening, while her babies squirmed and pushed at her soft furry flank.

After an hour of digging, when he was within two feet of the nest, the badger came against rocks, and the slit which guarded the nest, but which allowed entrance to the doe, was too narrow for him to squeeze through. When dawn came, he abandoned his efforts, and stamped grumpily away through the dew, soil-stained and hungry. Before nightfall the following day, the doe had dug a new burrow, and had removed her six babies to the new nest. Later a hunting stoat entered the old burrow, and chattered with rage and frustration at finding it empty, although still warm and smelling of rabbit.

That winter a hedgehog hibernated in the old burrow, and emerged covered in the fluff that the doe had stripped from her chest, when first she lined the nest for her young. Then a weasel raised her kitts there, and afterwards, for a long time, the burrow lay empty, with a spider's web across the door. Another rabbit came, and dug beyond the site of the first nest. Here she raised her young, and many generations of rabbits made their first appearance into the sunlight from the hole by the river bank. Then came a day when the fields and woodlands of France were littered with the corpses of rabbits, blind and swollen-faced, and soon the plague spread to England. Once more a spider spun his web across the entrance to the hole.

Syla adopted the burrow, for it was warm and dry, and sited conveniently between the two pools. Close by was a fallen ash, and Syla liked to sleep in a fork of the ash, secure in the knowledge that if danger threatened she could gain shelter immediately in the burrow. Thus, when she heard the barking of the dog, she watched inquiringly from her perch on the stump, ready for flight, but not unduly alarmed.

Along the twisty badger path came a young woman, tall and fair-haired, and as she walked she threw sticks for the dog, a tiny white and brown terrier, rough of coat and short legged. She and her pet had recently come to live in a cottage near the farm, and this bright morning in December, as the sun melted the frost and lit the golden gravel of the river, she had been tempted to explore the cleave.

In her preoccupation at viewing the once familiar form of a human after so long a time, Syla lingered a moment too long, forgetting that the burrow lay between her and the dog. As she ran towards it the terrier spotted her and gave chase, his joyous barking rising to fever pitch. Syla beat him easily to the burrow, and once inside, turned to see what was happening. For a moment the terrier paused, his bulk blocking the light as he scratched at the burrow, sniffing loudly. Then, as Syla pushed on deeper into the tunnel, the dog followed, grunting and puffing as he forced his way in. Syla slipped through the slit in the rocks and turned again, pressed against the wall of the outer nest, and waited.

The terrier reached the slit in the rocks, scented the strong musk of the frightened mink, and growled menacingly. Then he pressed his muzzle to the slit, found the widest part, and tried to push through. He was young and fit, without an ounce of spare flesh, so his head and shoulders made the gap easily. So did his chest, and only the bones of his pelvic girdle proved too bulky to pass through the rock. Unfortunately for the dog, the slit in the rock was wider at the top than at the bottom, and as he twisted to allow his hips to pass through, he slid down the crack, becoming permanently wedged.

Syla, prudently sheltering now in the inner nest, heard his growls turn to yelps of pain, and grow to screams of anguish as the sharp rock tore at his tender skin. Outside the burrow the woman listened also, becoming frantic with worry as the screams died away to muffled whimpers. Then there was no sound at all, only the song of the river under the December sun. The woman turned, and ran back up the cleave, stumbling over the rocks, tearing her stockings and cutting her hands and knees.

From time to time Syla emerged to survey the situation, but always she retreated, back into the nest. As long as she remained hidden the terrier lay quiet, but at the sight of her he would raise his head, snarling and showing his teeth, while he scrabbled frantically at the rocks and floor of the burrow with claws which were now torn and blood-stained. Syla debated whether or not to rush at the crack, for above the terrier there was room for her to escape. Her nerve was not equal to the task, however, and each time she retired out of the way.

The extension, the inner nest, eased the situation for both mink and dog. Had Syla been confined, cornered, in close proximity to the terrier, she might have attacked, tearing at eyes, ears, and nose in a desperate attempt to kill the dog. In all probability she would have failed, and been crushed between the back-breaking jaws of the larger animal. The distance between them prevented her nerve from giving way. Eventually, as the hours passed, and the position did not alter, she curled up and went to sleep:

She awoke to fresh fear, to the sounds of muffled shouting, to the frantic yelping of the dog, and dull thuds on the earth.

After the young woman had left the burrow where the terrier lay trapped, she had hurried as fast as she could to the farm, where she had gasped out her story to the farmer. He listened, outwardly sympathetic, inwardly sardonic, but stirred by an appeal for help from a pretty stranger. He collected mattock and spade, crowbar and felling axe, glad of an excuse to break the monotony of the farm, and hopeful of a pound or two reward.

Together they set off down the cleave, and when they reached the burrow the farmer threw off his coat, and lay down on the ground, reaching down into the burrow. He could feel nothing, so he took out his knife and cut a long bramble, trimming off the thorns, except for about six inches at one end. This end he inserted into the hole, pushing it gently in until, when he had barely a foot of bramble left, he felt resistance. He twirled the bramble round and round in his hand several times, and then withdrew it, examining the thorny end carefully. There, sure enough, were white hairs clinging to the thorns.

Now he knew where to dig. Laying the bramble on the ground, in line with the lie of the burrow, he marked the spot and began to break the turf with his mattock. It was these thuds which awoke Syla, while the terrier, feeling the touch of the bramble, and hearing the voice of his mistress, grew hysterical and started to struggle once more.

Soon the farmer struck the rocks which held him, and, as the farmer located the crack with his bar, loose earth began to fall. Before long the dog's hindquarters came into view, and soon the terrier was in his mistress's arms, licking her face and wriggling in ecstasy. The farmer watched this performance for a moment, and then returned to the hole, anxious to discover what had attracted the dog in the first place. He imagined it would be a rabbit, for there were a few about, hardy survivors of the plague. If it was, the sooner it was knocked on the head the better. He lay down once more and reached down into the hole, waving his arm about and groping wildly.

Syla's nerve held until the farmer actually touched her flank with his thumb. Then she attacked, screaming fear and hatred, sinking her teeth hard into the fleshy base of his thumb. Next moment she was flying through the air, bruised against the rocks, out into the light and cold of the winter afternoon, as the farmer pulled his hand from the hole. Syla's ribs cracked as the farmer grasped her round the waist with his free hand, and Syla changed her grip, biting the back of the hand that gripped her. Instantly the hand released its grip, and Syla, eyes closed, held grimly on as the farmer ran to the river. She felt the water close blissfully over her head as the farmer dipped his hand in the river, and, letting go, she twisted away like an eel and swam swiftly away downstream, across to the other side. Rocks and stones crashed into the undergrowth all round her as she raced away, and behind her the shouts of the farmer, the screams of the woman, and the hysterical yapping of the dog, gradually died away.

# 7 Ice Chains

THE wind, which had blown fresh and strong from the west, weakened and fell, dying with soft, breathless sighs among the dark caverns of the trees. The earth lay still, mute, awaiting the coming of the cold. Grey mist hung in the woods, and the sun was hidden by a thin veil of high cold cloud, while all around the smell of rotting leaves stung acrid and bitter in the nostrils. Quietly, without fuss, the animals made their preparations for survival in the weeks that were to follow, following the time-tested ritual that had guaranteed the survival of the species, if not of every individual.

The badger didn't bother to get up. His nocturnal outings grew shorter and shorter, his appetite less and less, his lethargy more pronounced, until at last, for twenty-three out of the twenty-four hours, he slept, deep under the ground. He slept, and he drowsed, but there was no true hibernation. He could be awakened at any time, in full possession of his faculties. Verrick the squirrel spent long hours asleep, snug in the warmth of his drey, high in a hollow tree. From time to time he would emerge, around noon, to hunt for the nuts he had buried so haphazardly in the autumn. There was no need for him to remember where he had hidden them. His nose located them unerringly as they lay an inch or so below the leaf-mould. If the ground was frozen, however, he stayed in hiding, preferring to go without food rather than waste energy in fruitless searching.

Other mammals, the bats, the dormice, the hedgehogs, were more thorough in their arrangements. Like the reptiles and amphibians which were now hidden away, out of reach of the frost, these small mammals went into hibernation. Breathing almost ceased. Body temperature dropped to a point where life would cease to exist had not each individual cell of the body renounced for the moment its need for nourishment and purification. The tiny heart beat, once every ten seconds, supplied the bare needs of the cells for existence, and the sluggish liver drew frugally on the supply of fat which had been hoarded to feed the body during this time. With so little energy being dissipated, the needs of the body were slight. The brain, serving no protective purpose during this time, ceased to record impressions or emotions, and lay inactive. Only the small monitor which controlled the life force ticked quietly away, preserving life.

Still, in the silence and the grey light, the woodlands were alive with movement. Here the trees and shrubs offered shelter, and a slightly higher air temperature than the open fields. Here the river offered moisture, and small birds flocked to the refuge. Blue tits and great tits shared the oaks. The blue tits needed to find at least one pupating insect, hidden among the twigs, every three seconds, if they were to find enough nourishment to survive. The great tits had the advantage of size and strength, but the blue tits could work among the smaller twigs, which would not bear the weight of the larger tits. The great tits stayed among the higher branches, and the blue tits kept to the lower, so, by and large, there was no competition.

Wrens were everywhere, relying, like the other birds, on their feathers to insulate them against the cold. Between their skin and the outer air there was a temperature drop of eighty degrees, but the fierce heat of the body metabolism needed constant stoking, if it were not to drop too low. At night the wrens packed together, twenty or thirty at a time, in order to conserve body heat, and survive long enough for daylight to come, and allow them to start stoking the tiny, fierce fires again.

For several days the air hung still, while at night the stars burned brilliantly in the cold sky. Frost bit into the earth, and each day seemed more reluctant to release its hold. The sun lacked the power to undo the work of the night, and it did not rise high enough above the horizon. White hoar lay in the shelter of the hills and boulders, at the foot of the oaks and along the sides of the hedges.

Then the sear grasses and the withered reeds trembled as the wind started to blow, this time from the east, cold and dry, driving before it in silent and inexorable majesty the blue-grey feathery-tipped clouds, endless legions of the frost battalions, the killer black frost, which left no pall of frozen moisture, no white hoar, no trace of its passing, only a land bound in chains.

Syla felt nothing of the cold. Her thick dark pelt insulated her so effectively, and her active metabolism so warmed her extremities, that even when a lace edge of ice began to form along the river, she still swam daily, feeding now more and more on trout, as eels vanished into the mud and gravel, frogs slept as if dead, and voles grew fewer, less active. She ranged farther afield, exploiting her new-found hunting skill and her intimate knowledge of the river in a daily quest for food which, with each successive dawn, grew just a little harder. Slowly, almost imperceptibly, she lost weight, although suffering no physical discomfort, either from cold or hunger. The fat she had accumulated during the autumn now served to maintain her physical well being, and helped to fire the metabolism increased by the effort of combating the cold.

Again the wind changed, veering northward, increasing in force, growing perceptibly milder, while the sky, which had been high and grey, seemed to pack down, lighter, sulphurous-yellow. Then again the wind died, and white flakes drifted down, at first few and intermittently, then faster, faster, so that their numbers began to cover the ground, and the distant hills were blotted out by the whirling, twirling dervish dance of the snow flakes. All day it snowed, and at night. Then towards dawn the wind rose again, distorting the exquisite geometrical design of the flakes, breaking them into small fragments, and hurling them across the face of the land so that they could only fall in the path of objects that had broken the force of the wind. Here, in the eddies of wind currents, they piled in great drifts, blocking roads, burying sheep and cattle, isolating farms, and marooning travellers.

With the dawn the wind dropped, but no sun shone to bring warmth to the landscape. Birds huddled in disconsolate flocks in the wind-bitten branches of the thorns, their plumage vivid in its colour against the white. Rabbits floundered, bewildered and helpless in this unreal world, and a fox stood belly deep, his face and ears frosted with white, and his angry brush sweeping the snow, as he stared with frustrated rage after a fleeting cock pheasant.

Dusk fell, and the frost bit deeper into the land, while owls sailed on frightened nervous wings, anxiously searching for the voles that lay buried, safe in their burrows under the turf. The owls turned instead to the stackyards and bullock pens, searching among the environs of the farmhouse, and visiting the gardens of the village, for the rats and mice that had moved in to live with man at the beginning of the winter. The foxes made their rounds as usual, padding under the silent stars. The dog fox barked his soft, double call, and from across the valley the vixen answered with a scream, for now the blood of the fox demanded more than food. So the foxes sought their mates, and fought their battles of possession on the frozen hills. They hunted too, however, and in the morning the signs were plain to see, as blood, and fur or feathers littered the tumbled snow.

Syla, overwhelmed and quite silly with delight and wonderment at the discovery of the snow, played most of the night. Rolling, diving, somersaulting into snowdrifts, making snowballs which she pushed along with her chest, sliding down the river bank and racing back up, eager for the thrill of another exhilarating toboggan ride, it was almost dawn before her hunger drove her to hunt. By then fatigue had made her clumsy, and it was well into the morning before she killed and ate. Fortunately the fish was a large one, near half a pound in weight, and long before she had consumed the entire carcase she crawled away, gorged and sleepy, pausing only for a drink before curling up to sleep for a few hours.

The remains of the fish were left on the gravel spit where Syla had breakfasted, rapidly turning to ice. They were seen almost simultaneously by a young rat, journeying along the terraces under the river bank, and a carrion crow, flying up stream towards the farm. The rat reached the fish first, and was already biting into the frozen flesh when the crow landed on the gravel beside him. Hunger made the rat desperate, and with a squeal and a show of yellow hatchet teeth he foolishly disputed possession of his prize with the crow. The rat died suddenly and violently as a sledge-hammer of a bill drove into his skull, and the crow dined well on fish and rat. So far he, and others of his tribe, had found little hardship from the cold.

The cold continued, and the wind blew again from the east, strong and remorseless, so that the weather began to take its toll. Ispi the kingfisher was dead, an azure cross staining the snow, while redwings, their faith in migration betrayed and their strength spent, sat waiting to die, or lay crumpled in their snowy graves, their wings their headstones. Here the scavengers found them, but a bird that has died of starvation makes poor fare. A mouthful of feathers, a morsel of bone, a little frozen tissue, certainly not an adequate meal for a hungry hunter. Each long night took its toll of victims, and now they fell with increasing frequency. Many of the birds were victims, not of cold or starvation, but of poison they had absorbed during the summer. They had eaten insects or seeds contaminated with insecticide, which they had stored harmlessly in their fat, and now that they had been forced to metabolize their fat, the accumulated poison had entered their bloodstreams, destroying their weakened nervous systems.

Syla found and ate several of these corpses. She too was absorbing organochlorines, from poisoned birds, from the trout, from voles. No animal, or bird, or reptile, or fish, no insect or grub was entirely free. Spread upon the land, it was re-absorbed into the atmosphere, to fall again in the rain, to lie in the mud of the rivers. Here waterborn insects found it, and accumulated a little, three or four parts per million, in their systems. Trout ate the insects, and accumulated ten parts per million. Syla had perhaps thirty parts per million in her system, while fish-eating birds absorbed a hundred or more parts per million, before they died. Those that did not passed the insecticide on in their eggs, so that the eggs did not hatch, but lay cold and infertile in the nest.

The nights were lighter now, as the moon waxed and shone over the suffering land. It shed its cold brilliance over the river, slower and more silent now in its ice fetters, over the thinly populated woodland, with its few survivors struggling against death, and over the cruel, arctic wastes of the barren cleave. It shone on boulder and stone, casting purple moonshadows and illuminating a large white shape on the edge of a rocky crag.

The white shape, which might have been a snow drift, suddenly moved, and detached itself from the crag, flying on soft wide wings, low over the surface of the cleave. The snowy owl had arrived the previous dusk, crossing the channel from the continent and, weakened from weeks of fasting, blown off course by the strong wind. Thus it had travelled hundreds of miles instead of tens of miles, and, although it had no exact prescience of its fate, it realized instinctively that if it did not feed that night, by the following night it would be dead. In desperation it quartered the cleave, dropping nearer and nearer the woodland, and the river.

The owl reached the clearing by the salmon pool, and lighted on the bare branch of an ash tree. Here it waited, where it could see both banks of the river, up and down stream, for already it knew that it was too weak, too weary, for sustained flight. Its eyes scanned the white ground beneath it, the brilliant pupils dilated wide, and able to discern, even in the dim light of the moon, each individual snow crystal, sparkling with frost diamonds. The owl's ears, huge and sensitive, hidden, yet aided by rosettes of short stiff feathers, were alert for any slight sound. Constantly, to aid hearing and vision, the owl turned its head from side to side. The rest of its body remained still, statuesque, waiting.

A slight scratching came from downstream, and the owl ceased its head movements, elongating its neck in the direction of the sound. A dark blob detached itself from the shadows of a fallen holly, travelled a few paces with a curious looping gait, then stopped, scratching at the snow. Then the shape grew nearer, elongated, snake like, preoccupied with its searching of the snow-covered ground, and oblivious of the waiting owl, taut and crouching, high above.

The owl moved twice. Once, as the mink passed under the tree, turning on the branch in preparation for its spring, and then, almost immediately, dropping with outstretched talons, to land on the back of the mink, just behind its head. Whether the owl misjudged its attack, or whether the mink checked in the nick of time, no one could say. One foot completely missed the mink. The other half circled the mink's head, failing to obtain a secure grip, and lacerating one ear, and part of the animal's cheek. With a scream of mingled pain and rage the mink flung itself at the owl, now helpless and floundering in the snow, and succeeded in obtaining a grip on the owl's head, just at the side of its throat. The owl flapped and tried to turn, to bring its talons into play, but the mink, a strong young male, backed swiftly away, dragging the owl after him, and shifting his grip with lightning speed, until he had the owl by the throat.

The mink, whose name was Motik, drank some of the blood of the owl, and ate a little of the stringy, rancid flesh, before moving on. He had journeyed far, having escaped from a mink farm on the sea coast a month previously. He was to have been killed, and his pelt sent to London, with those of his brothers and sisters, but he had twisted from the farmer's grasp at the last moment. He had hidden among a pile of empty boxes, and the farmer, busy with the other mink, had ignored him for the moment. By nightfall, when the farmer went in search of him, Motik had changed his hiding place, eventually making good his escape by walking out of the farm gate, while the staff of the farm searched the mink pens in vain.

He had left the coast, which was overpopulated and noisy, following the river upstream, past the pollution of the town, and over the lush fields of the lowlands. He was tempted to stay in the woodland, but the encounter with the owl, and the pain of his torn ear and face, drove him on, past the bridge, but following the course of the main river, instead of turning up the small stream.

In the morning Syla found the remains of the owl, and read the story of the fight. With hackles raised, she followed the tracks of the male mink, but beyond the bridge she did not venture.

# 8 Thaw

THERE was no moment of dawn. A pattern grew out of the darkness, a pattern which revealed shadow where once there was none. Pattern became form, and form revealed shape, and the land lay as it had the night before, frozen, ice-chained, and lifeless. Above the trees, the sky was changed. Clouds hung low, swollen, pendulous, and suddenly a breeze drifted through the branches of the thorns, a soft, warm breeze. As if in answer the snow began, great wet flakes, falling rapidly, without drifting.

So came the thaw, as suddenly and dramatically as the bursting of a dam. The breeze grew to a wind, gusting in from the west, and turning the snowflakes into a torrential downpour of rain. The rain and the melted snow was swept off the frozen land, racing off the hilltops and down into the stream. The river thundered and roared, foaming down among the boulders, icy cold and capped with snow broth, the water strangely clear and ice-blue. Flotsam drifted on the surface, broken reeds and straw, empty bottles, wood, sticks and branches, drowned chickens, a dead sheep, slowly eddying round as the current slowed at the salmon pool.

As the frost began to melt, as the clouds packed down over the hills to condense on the cold surface of stone and earth, so the moisture began to permeate everywhere. Syla woke to find the walls of her sleeping quarters, deep among a clitter of boulders, running with icy water. Outside, movement was well nigh impossible in the soft wet snow, and the river ran bank-high, unfishable, and dangerous. Syla retired once more, even wetter, shivering, cold, hungry, and ill-tempered.

For two days and a night the cold rain and mist persisted, but on the evening of the second day the rain stopped, the mist cleared, and as a warm southerly breeze rocked the top of the ash tree, a blackbird sang a few faltering notes. Within a week the frost was forgotten, and the inhabitants of the wood, those which had survived, began with much bustle and toil to make up for lost time, and to prepare for the coming of the new generation. Above the tor, where his faithful mate sat brooding a clutch of four eggs, Arak the raven tumbled in ecstasy as he flew through the mild air. Down in the wood the robin sang his territory song, repeatedly attacking a hen which persisted in ignoring his threats, until at last he realized his errors.

Long days in March, cold and dry, were still to follow, days when the awakening earth was to settle back to sleep in the arms of winter, but for the moment it was the false spring. The hazel catkins glittered gold in the pale light, primroses shone like pale stars, and violets peeped shyly from among the withered fern. Each day grew a little longer, and each noon the sun rose a little higher. Already the world was greener, for it was the turn of the tide, and now began the first soft lappings, the faintest stirrings of the great swelling flood which was to surge upward and onward, finally to rush into high summer.

The frost had not been wholly harmful. It had done good, swelling the soil, aerating and crumbling it down to a fine tilth. It had softened the hard shells of the seeds, allowing moisture to permeate and stimulate the growth of the plant. It had broken down the withered remains of last year's growth, so that it would rot down to form food for the coming carpet of leaf and stem. Here and there it had killed, biting deep into the heart of a tree, so that the root hairs would no longer take up water from the soil, and the leaves would not form. In death the tree would continue to support life, for insects would feed on the rotting pulp of the timber, birds would seek out the fat grubs which bored through the bark, and as the decaying heart of the tree became hollow, many animals would come to live there, mice and voles, bats and owls, woodpeckers, squirrels, nuthatches, and even snakes. Even when the tree fell, it would still offer shelter and food, and a slow worm would live underneath.

Syla found such a tree, dry and hollow, with a narrow entrance each end, and a floor of dry, dusty wood. The discovery strangely excited her, she knew not why, and she visited the tree regularly, although making no attempt to sleep there. Inside she discovered the skull of a weasel, which had crawled there to die after being mauled by a fox. Sometimes she played with the skull, and it was always the first thing she checked on when she visited the log.

The fishing was poor. The trout were lean and hungry after the twin ordeal of spawning and frost. They hung, lean as wolves in the clear water, and grew increasingly wary of Syla as she came to hunt. There was no shortage of voles, however, and Syla, thin now, hungry, and considerably fitter than when she had escaped from the farm, grew more catholic in her diet. Frogs were emerging from where they had hibernated, and were making their way to their traditional spawning grounds. Lizards, too, were beginning to stir, appearing briefly at midday, when the sun shed its gentle warmth on the rocks. Snails hung in great clusters, each shell sealed to prevent moisture loss until such time as there were sufficient green plants to feed the snails. Syla sampled all these foods, including the earthworms, which once she had eaten and despised. Now she was not so fastidious, and rarely went hungry for long.

One evening in late February, as the setting sun hung on the dark shoulder of the cleave, gilding the tips of the willow branches, and staining the granite rocks with streaks of coral, Syla stood on a rock overlooking the pool below the steps. Flies were hatching on the surface of the water, and the small trout were feeding greedily, taking the nymphs as they struggled to reach the surface, or picking off the newly hatched flies as they broke away from their imago. Syla watched, as the soft twilight stole through the trees. A bat fluttered down, sweeping round in a wide circle, now lost in the shadows, now winging low over Syla's head. A wren, greatly daring, flew out from the rocks, hovering clumsily in the air and striving to grasp the flies with gaping beak. An owl called, softly, and this seemed to arouse Syla, to remind her that time was passing. Quietly, she slipped into the water at the foot of the pool.

She swam a few strokes, and then dived, her neck outstretched, her forefeet pressed tightly to her chest, swimming strongly underwater with vigorous kicks of her hind legs. Dimly she was aware of the wavering pebbles below her, and the wide arc of light that was the surface of the river. Ahead of her she could see the tails of two, three, then four trout, and she sank lower, suddenly thrusting upwards, slashing at the underbelly of the biggest.

She missed, and the trout dived away, down into the depths of the pool, where the light was dimmer and the current, foaming over the rocks, plunged in a silver shower of bubbles which were scattered and broken, filtering up through the clear water. The trout shot under a ledge of rock, pressed hard against the stone, and waited, fearful, as Syla came slowly along, nosing the crack where the trout lay. The fish panicked and turned, betraying his presence by a golden flash of flank, and Syla spun to meet him, teeth clashing on scale and fin, sliding over the trout, then sinking into firm flesh that twisted and squirmed in her grasp. A small pink cloud grew round the struggling trout, and drifted away downstream, to be followed by three scales.

Syla kicked upwards and broke surface, lying on her back with the trout in her jaws. Gently she drifted downstream, kicking occasionally to bring herself nearer the bank, so that by the time she reached the lower lip of the pool she had but a yard to cover to reach the bank. Here, on a narrow spit of sand, she ate the trout, starting at the tail, and crunching skin and bone, scale and flesh, holding the meat with her front paws, and tearing it with sharp white teeth. A badger came padding along the riverside path and paused, sniffing and peering through the gloom. At his scrutiny Syla froze, her jaws half open, recognizing the badger as harmless but not entirely trusting him.

The badger was lonely. His mate had given birth that day to three silver-haired cubs, and when he had invited her out she had driven him away, snapping and snarling, until at length he had left the sett, to go foraging alone. The mink, however, was alien to him, offering no hope of companionship, so he wandered on, grumbling a little to himself, and, after pausing to reach to his full height and make his mark on a scratching tree, he disappeared out of sight.

Syla slipped back into the water, paddling on the surface and dipping her head down under water, peering into the gloom. A writhing ribbon of silver, far down among the mud and leaves of an eddy, came winking up to her and she kicked downwards in a joyous dive; an eel, the first she had seen since the long cold spell had begun. She caught it across the middle of the back and felt its head rap against her neck. The tail curled round her, and she brought up one paw to free herself of the entangling embrace. Then, rising to the surface, she bit the eel in half. Still in the water, dog paddling, she ate some of the front half, meantime watching the tail end drift away, diving after it and retrieving it just as it seemed it would be drawn into the white water and washed away downstream.

She was thus engaged, half feeding, half playing with the eel and chasing the ever shrinking fragments down the pool, when she heard the call of the male mink. It came echoing across the water, rising above the murmur of the stream, soft, urgent, compelling, the rolling, purring, love call of her kind. Syla hung in the water, alert, watchful, but nervous, and the remains of the eel drifted away, forgotten in the half light.

Motik stood on a flat rock at the head of the pool, peering down at Syla in the water, and once again he called. Then, as Syla swam slowly towards him he ran into the water, broke surface and waited. Syla drew near, noted his size, thrilled as she realized he was twice as big as she. She saw, but paid no heed to the great scar that ran across his head, over one ear, and down his cheek. She noticed his manner, however, and saw that it was gentle, friendly, anxious. Thus reassured, she came closer, but at the last moment she kicked aside, and swam strongly away downstream.

Motik followed, and together they played through the long spring night, swimming, rolling, wrestling in mock battle, playing endless games of tag in and out of the water, and racing across the short grass of the clearing. Continually Motik sang to her, and the magic of his song began slowly to hypnotize Syla, so that she grew less boisterous, less quick, feeling more and more a delicious languor which lulled away her fears of danger.

Still she was not quite ready to submit to his demands,

and the moment his attentions became too ardent she would shy away, first petulant, then, as he insisted, savage with sudden, white-hot anger. At the sound of her screams, and the display of her teeth and jaws, Motik grew prudent and respectful, and towards dawn, his passion cooling with fatigue and hunger, the two mink hunted together.

The grey ghosts of the trees shone faintly through the mist, as the dawn, sombre yet beautiful in robes of softest pink and deep dove-grey, crept down the hillside and lingered at the pool. The two mink stood side by side, reluctant to part, yet not knowing what to do. Motik moved a few paces upstream, then turned, looking back for Syla to follow. Syla stood and stared, wishing Motik would stay, yet longing for the warmth and security of her own home among the rocks. So, regretfully, the two animals parted, and soon both were deep in slumber, three miles apart, but each crying and trembling as, in their dreams, they relived the joys and excitements of the night.

# 9 Conception

SPRING, which had awakened so smiling and full of promise, shivered in the east wind and slipped back into an uneasy sleep in the arms of the winter. No bird sang, no insects hatched on the still surface of the salmon pool. The primroses lay dormant in their green rosettes of leaves, and the frogs lay inert in the mud at the bottom of the field pond. The lizards crawled back under the stones.

Then came the west wind, shouting and roaring over the moors, wet with rain drawn from the warm Atlantic, which he flung in great shining sheets over the patient land. When he had done, the sun shone with a new warmth, a new power, so that the racing clouds scowled black with anger, towering over the purple twigs of the leafless birches. Next morning, the blackbird sang again in the ash tree, and the bubbling call of the curlew echoed from across the marsh field.

After their first meeting, Syla waited for many nights near the pool below the steps. He did not come, and gradually, Syla forgot. Sometimes she would wait wistfully, listening for the soft caress of his call, and once she marked the scent of his passing. As time went by, and the awakening world of spring brought each night new and exciting distractions, she thought about him less and less.

The nights were full of magic. Soft stirrings and whisperings, tiny movements on the leaf-spattered ground. The soft air was pungent with scents as countless tiny mammals made their bustling preparations for the year to come. Their numbers were legion. On them depended the great pyramid of life, for they, and their offspring, formed the staple diet of all the larger predators, owl and hawk, buzzard and crow, jay and magpie, fox and badger, stoat, weasel, mink and otter, polecat, pine marten and wild cat, all of which were soon to raise a family, a litter of young which would need a surplus of easy prey, if they were to survive the first few difficult months of life.

So the providers worked to make themselves the sacrifice. The bank vole and the short-tailed vole, the long-tailed field mouse, the shrew, eschewed by the mammals, but eaten by the birds, the ubiquitous brown rat, and, in lesser numbers, the pigmy shrew, the water shrew, the dormouse, the harvest mouse and the water vole, all were busy. They converted the raw material of seeds and vegetation, insects and grubs, into a compact little unit of high quality protein. Eaten entire, the vole comprised all the essential needs of the predator, and was therefore in great demand. Ill equipped to defend itself as an individual, the vole survived as a species because it bred so fast. Sexually mature in five weeks, giving birth in another three weeks, and pregnant immediately after the young had been born, there were never less than a hundred voles at any one time to the acre, and sometimes as many as four hundred or more.

Without them, life could not go on. Left to themselves, they would inherit, and destroy, the earth. By their numbers, they controlled the number of the predators, so that if, for some reason, the voles did not breed, then the young of the predators starved. If the vole population increased, then the foxes and the owls, the stoats and the weasels, flocked to the feast, and so a pattern was maintained.

Syla knew nothing of this, but she made her contribution to the ecology of the woodland. Trout were lean and few, so the mink turned to the warm-blooded mammals of the wood and their dying cries were lost in the cries of countless other voles, voles new born, voles dying in the grip of tooth and claw, a flowing sea of life. Syla needed a mixed diet, fish and flesh. She needed small meals, at frequent intervals, and her diet needed to be rich in minerals and vitamins. She got these from the fur and feather of the small animals she killed, from the liver, heart and other organs. Fortunately, she was well equipped to hunt, and, equally fortunately, she was small, so her appetite was soon satisfied.

Whether she fished or not, most nights she swam. She loved water, whether it was the great limpid stretch of the salmon pool, the turbulent white water of the race below the steps, or even a tiny trickle escaping through the woodland, tinkling down amid the rock and ferns, eager to join the main river. One night she lay alone, sprawled on a lichen-covered rock beside a long, narrow pool, a mere cleft in the rock, where the water flowed silently, without ripple. Starlight shone on the black velvet of the water, great amethysts of light without form or substance, which Syla took for her playthings, striving to catch them in her tiny jaws.

Then the starlight danced in the cold water of the pool, shivering and sparkling, as it did now. Syla watched from the rock, as out of the shimmering stars a wide V formed, stretching from bank to bank. In the middle of the V a dark blob, which grew larger, nearer, until with a chirrup, Motik arrived at her feet.

Now a thousand stars shattered into tiny fragments, and the black waters of the pool burst into white fire as the two animals played out their happiness. Then Syla went away downstream, and Motik followed, keeping close behind as Syla led him through splashet and trickle, over moss and stone, along birch log and through alder thicket, running in the night until to her the stars and the river, the dark flowing water and the soft blackness of the night were one with the song of Motik.

At last, on the short turf of the clearing, where the trees were a tunnel to the skies, she submitted to the magic of the song and the soft languor in her body. In her weakness she felt the grip of Motik's teeth on the skin at the back of her neck. With eyes closed she submitted to the embrace of his forelegs, pinning her on her side and drawing her to him. The song went on, and with it the song of the river, and so there was no pain and no fear, and through the strange alchemy of love an hour passed, and there was no time.

Sleep came, and when she awoke the trees shone pale in

the first light of dawn. Motik lay a little apart, watching her, and she approached him shyly, tentatively, hesitant to touch him until he rolled on to his back, inviting her to wrestle and play. Later they hunted together, and when the sun was high they slept in the hollow roots of an oak, the holt of an otter long since dead.

For three nights and two days Syla and Motik stayed in the holt, playing together, hunting together, and three times Syla succumbed to the magic of Motik's song. On the third night, as the moon was rising above the black shoulder of the cleave, the two mink played in the starlit pool where they had met three nights before. Here the moon joined them, and they both tried in vain to catch this strange crescent-shaped fish, that melted in their mouths and bobbed mockingly before them. At last Syla drifted downstream, and almost immediately spotted an eel, which burrowed itself under some stones in the shallows. Syla worked frantically, turning over stones and digging among the gravel in an endeavour to come to grips with her prize. So it was that she did not hear the call of Motik, did not see him depart. He lingered long in the distance, looking back over his shoulder and calling with all the ardour he possessed, but Syla was engrossed with her eel.

Motik slipped away, fully intending to return, moving upstream with the curious snake-like gait of his kind. He was heading for the chicken run on the edge of the farm-yard, for in the past he had caught many rats there, and he was anxious to show Syla the rich hunting that was his. Since she wouldn't come, he would hunt alone, and perhaps later she would join him. If not, he would return to her with the dawn.

When the dawn did come, Motik lay on his side, his forepaw crushed and broken in the iron jaws of a gin, illegally set by the farmer for the rats that had been robbing him of eggs. Here the farmer found him, three hours later, and Motik screamed with rage, slashing with reddened fangs at the boot which stirred him in his wretchedness. So the farmer, who had been about to crush the life out of Motik with his heel, whistled instead for the terrier, and stood silent, smoking nervously, as the terrier did his work.

Syla slept alone in the otter's holt, unaware of the death of Motik, or of the changes that were taking place within her. She had conceived. The hard days of winter, coupled with the sparsity of food, had removed all the surplus fat from her and rendered her in the peak of condition, so that the lengthening of the days and the sudden flush of rich feed had stimulated her glands to full production. On her meeting with Motik, she was fitter than she had ever been in all her life, yet it was the magic of Motik's song that had stimulated her ovaries into function. Their first mating had left her barren, for Motik was hardly in his full vigour. On the second she had conceived, but still the greater part of the miracle of life was yet to be fulfilled.

The fertilized ova lay within her womb, but as yet they were dormant, inert. Other mammals, once they have conceived, accept the fertile ova, which become implanted in the wall of the womb and begin to receive nourishment from the blood supply of the parent. With Syla, along with other members of the weasel tribe, this did not happen. The time for mating was passed, but, as a precaution against a sudden return of winter, as an insurance against hard times to come, the eggs rested, protected, yet not developing, so that no one could forecast when Syla would give birth.

March drifted lazily away, day following day, each one growing a little longer, a little warmer. All the feverish activity which was taking place, all the preparations which were going ahead were mostly hidden from view. Underground, in the warmth and darkness of the soil, all was being made ready for the time when the warmth of April would summon the first green blades above the surface. Seeds were soft and pliable, ready to burst into life. In the leafless trees, the sap was running, as the rootlets absorbed moisture from the soil, and carrying vital salts and minerals, together with essential nitrogen, up the trunk of the tree, along the branches, through the tiniest twigs, so that each leaflet could burst from the protection of its bud secure in the knowledge that its lifeline would not fail it. Before the advance of spring, the lines of communication were made secure.

As the first blowfly buzzed lazily round the carcase of a dead lamb, seeking to lay her neatly ordered rows of eggs, so the first queen wasp droned along the hedgebank, looking for a site where she could make her nest, and bring forth the grubs which she would feed on the flies which hatched from the dead lamb. As the moths began to flutter among the oaks, the bat gave birth to her single infant, which she would carry and feed until late summer. The croaking frogs sang in the chilly waters of the pond, and the masses of spawn sank to the bottom, to swell as it absorbed water, and finally to float near the surface, where the sun and light could bring it to life. The same warmth and light would produce the first growth of plankton, on which the tiny tadpoles would at first feed. Later, the plankton would also feed the small animal life which the maturing tadpoles would come to crave. Whether the spring came early or late, the timing would still be perfectly synchronized.

The opening day of the trout fishing season came, but no angler fought his way up the wilderness of the cleave. The trout were reckoned too small, too insignificant to be worth the effort, and so Syla was left in peace. On the first day of April, exactly fourteen days after her mating with Motik, and without being aware in the slightest degree that anything unusual was happening to her, Syla accepted the fertilized ova within her, and began to nourish them.

# 10 The Moor Burn

THE woodlands quickened and pulsed with new, thrusting life, but on the cleave winter still reigned. The wind blew cold among the tangled grey masses of rock, and the thin earth lay inactive beneath its umber cloak of bracken, crushed beneath the weight of winter snows. The bracken was not dead. Under the ground, safe from frost and drought, long roots stretched horizontally over the hill, and already the roots were thrusting blind, curling spears skywards, drawn by the small stimuli of light and warmth. The bracken was all powerful, strangling other growth by stealing nourishment and light, and safe from browsing animals because of its poisonous fronds.

Only the spring flowers, the bluebells and the wild

strawberries, benefited from the bracken. The bluebells used the blanket of dead fronds as a protection from the frost, and later the blooms enjoyed the dappled light and shade that the young fern fronds provided. Long before the bracken reached its full height, the time for the bluebells and strawberries was past, and the bracken could not harm them. When the growth of bracken was at its peak, only the climbing plants, like the bramble, could climb above the fern in search of the all important light.

Over the cleave, thrusting through the tangled waves of dead fronds, sweating in the sunlight in spite of the breeze, there came a boy. He was fifteen, perhaps, or sixteen, fair of face and complexion. Physically he was as near perfection as modern concepts of health and medicine could make him. Born with the assistance of asepsis and surgical skill, well nourished, immunized against disease, and exercised so that his body made full use of the benefits bestowed upon it, he could look forward to a life expectancy twice that of his forebears.

Mentally he was less well equipped. All natural hazards, which in a less sheltered environment might well have brought about his extinction as an individual, had been removed, and in a hundred ways he was protected from his own ignorance and folly. His brief period of education had been fully occupied with endeavours to fill his brain with essential knowledge and facts, information which would help to make him a useful unit of society, and enrich him personally for the role he was to play. Yet he lacked the ability to think without bias, to foresee, and to forestall. He could not appraise a situation in its widest terms, but only as it affected him. He was full of prejudices and clichés, forced upon him and hurriedly snatched up in his race to reach maturity. He accepted them because they were easier to assimilate than the tortuous processes of original thought, and since to his perpetual question 'Why?' there was always a glib and easy answer, it never occurred to him to explore further the riddles of the world around him.

He was the son of a farmer, and knew of 'good' land and 'bad' land. Good land was rich, fertile soil that was easily worked and yielded heavy crops. It made him wealthy. Bad land brought him no return for his labours, none that were immediately foreseeable, and any thought which he gave to the bad land was concerned directly with how to increase its fertility in terms of hard cash for himself. So as he walked over the cleave he glared at the bracken with hatred, and visualized the hill covered with rich green grass on which fat cattle and sheep grazed, and himself driving to market dressed in fine clothes, at the wheel of a fast car.

The light wind blew from the south, rippling up over the hill, and a buzzard – a bad bird because it occasionally killed lambs – hung in the clear blue sky. As it saw the boy it mewed softly, and swung away to the north, riding the wind and accelerating so that it was quickly out of sight. The boy wished he had brought his gun.

The bracken was tinder dry. It cloaked the hillside without a break, and only the rocks and scrub oaks stood out like tiny islands. The boy reached the limit of the cleave, where a low dry stone wall divided it from the rough upland pastures and the chain of woodlands that marked the course of the river. The wind blew away from him, up over the cleave. Here in the shelter of the wall the sun was hot. A wood ant scurried over the dry fern, bearing with it a tiny fragment of wood, material for the nest. The bracken crackled in the heat. A match would set it ablaze from end to end.

Nervously the boy looked around him. Below him the river sparkled amid purple twigs of birch and amber tops of oak. Before him the hill stretched golden to where it met the sky. A raven hung, nailed like a ragged black cross above the tor. The boy fumbled in his pocket, drew out a battered packet of cigarettes, and a box of matches. He knew that each year hill farmers practised the art of swaling; this consisted of burning the old and overgrown herbage to make room for the new. He knew that the destruction of the dead growth released minute amounts of fertilizer, lime, phosphates, potash and other salts, which would enrich the ground and feed the new growth. He also knew that properly, swaling should be carried out against the wind, fifty yards at a time, so that the fire was ever under control, never too fierce, and he knew that the lawful time for swaling was now past, and he could get into serious trouble. He lit his cigarette, weighing the legal position with the moral one. Two days ago he could have legally set light to the cleave. What difference could two days make? A match dropped here would carry the fire right across the hill, but there was nothing to spoil, no danger to stock or household, just a lot of old fern. It could catch fire by accident.

The match burned clear and steady in his fingers, its yellow flame scarcely flickering. He would drop the match. If the cleave caught alight it would burn. If the match went out, he would go away.

The tiny sliver of burning wood fell at his feet, and the yellow tongue of flame shrank and withered to nothing. The wood glowed red, and then the flame rose again, stretching upwards, consuming the unburnt wood of the match. The burning wood twisted, and the flame reached out, eager, questing, found a frond, consumed it, grew, leapt to another, divided, and divided yet again. Smoke began to rise, and the flames divided again and again, now crackling and hissing in their spiteful anger as they scythed into the feast of fern. Behind them they left a dreary black waste, a charred skeleton of the umber glory that once had been. The flames fanned out, climbing higher and higher, now rising and wavering waist high.

The boy, in sudden panic, tried to stamp them out, realized almost immediately that his efforts were fruitless and that he had cut off his retreat. He made his way back to the house by a long circuitous route, arriving home late for his dinner and in a bad temper.

As the full strength of the breeze caught the flames the fire began to leap ahead of itself. Great tongues of flame flickered and roared, then launched themselves into the air in front of the main red glow. A funeral pall of smoke reared above the hill, carrying with it glowing sparks, and delicate grey fragments of fern, reduced to carbon by the heat of the fire. A linnet crouched in uncomprehending terror on her nest in a gorse bush, sheltering her eggs by her body. Then the fire crackled around the stem of the bush, and the flames snaked upward to snatch her into their maw. The linnet flew away, badly scorched about the legs and wings, while the flames fell upon the nest reducing it to charred fragments. The eggs cracked and boiled, finally falling through the disintegrating nest, and were lost on the ground.

The badgers crouched in their setts, accustomed to the smell of smoke, and the stifling heat of the air that filtered down to them. Stoically they endured the discomfort, knowing that it would soon be past and that they were safe where they were. They knew too that after the fire there would be rich pickings on the barren cleave, for not every animal would escape the fire.

A slow worm was one of the first to die. It travelled some distance on the rim of the fire, twisting and turning as it sought the safety of a hole, or a crack in the rocks. The flames seemed to lift it on its way, until at last, blinded by the heat, it travelled into the heart of the fire, finally twisting into a tight knot before uncurling in its final freedom.

A great avalanche of flame engulfed the skylark as she waited for death, and her body, its tiny life snuffed out in a single heartbeat, fostered the doomed eggs for several hours more. Voles ran shrieking from their shallow runs, as the walls caved in on them in a raging mass of fire, They scurried over the charred embers, their fur alight, their eyes sightless, and their feet blistered and raw. Some died quickly, others huddled in misery, racked with pain and thirst, waiting without understanding for the arrival of the dark wings of death to carry them away.

Countless thousands of insects died, their bodies exploding out of the rigid case of chitin that enclosed them. Some died without knowing what killed them, as they hid on blade of grass or in hollow stem of bracken. Some flew up, and rose with the smoke cloud, carried upwards in a column of stifling heat and gas that destroyed wing and antenna, so that they fell, alive but helpless, on to an alien earth many miles away. Some flew into the heart of the inferno itself, and in an instant were reduced to the essential ash which would one day be recreated into sentient, living bodies. The ants toiled on, marching blindly into a death as purposeful and passionless as their life. Many thousands of insects survived, by the sheer chance of their locality, and in an incredibly short space of time they would repopulate the cleave. The dead would never be missed.

Millions of seeds, some of which had laid dormant for over fifty years, and which were about to germinate into life, were destroyed for ever. The bracken waited underground, safe in its impregnable fortress, and waited for its time. Most of the ash, the fertilizer, would go to feed the bracken. Sap boiled and bubbled in the twigs of young saplings, leaves curled and withered on the stems of the brambles, mosses and ferns, lichens and fungi, moulds and bacteria, all were reduced to the same basic ash. Sheep ticks, dormant among the tangled foliage of the gorse bushes, exploded in the heat, and a blowfly, trapped in the silken snare of a spider's web, gained its freedom a split second before it died.

The fire saw strange kinships. A weasel ran alongside a field vole, and a fox outpaced a hare. Grass snakes travelled in company with frogs and toads, while a merlin flew in unison with a flock of small birds. All fled from the common enemy, and only Arak, the raven, hunched on a rocky outcrop of the tor, where his mate brooded a pair of hideous, scaly fledglings, remained aloof. As the raven watched the blaze, memories filtered back into his evil black brain, memories of past fires, intermingled with mind pictures of battles fought on the soil of France, where once he had wandered, and a recollection of a dead body, that of an airman, here on the cleave. To Arak, death was life, and he had lived long.

Syla awoke to a dusk lurid with the flickering red light on the hill. From time to time, as the flames rose, the trees would be lit in outline against a starless sky, and the warm air was rank with the smell of smoke. A carpet of ash fouled the woodland floor, and above the chatter of the river came the sullen growl and roar of the blaze. Nervous, agitated, Syla followed the familiar path by the river, and found the wood flung into confusion by the influx of numberless animals, all homeless and lost, all seeking shelter, some maimed and burnt, some injured by other animals. With them had come visiting predators, stoat and weasel, hill fox and polecat, killing and plundering as the helpless prey blundered about in the unfamiliar woodland.

Syla took her share in the killing, and soon she slaughtered indiscriminately, without any desire to feed. Corpses littered the paths and clearings as her blood lust grew, and the bloodshed lasted until dawn. Then, as the weary killers returned to their beds, the scavengers took over. Jay and crow, magpie and buzzard, the jackdaws, the starlings and the heron, began their pleasurable task of clearing away all signs of the carnage. The heron was especially pleased, for he had a nest, one of three in a small heronry a mile downstream, in which two gawky, long-legged youngsters clamoured to be fed. On this day the heron filled their crops with ease, and was able to take a bit of a holiday. On the cleave Arak sat hunched on his favourite granite spur, while the sun warmed his back, surveying the blackened surface of the hill. Soon the vegetation would return, spreading across the ground like a green mist. For a moment Arak was almost invisible, a black bird of death in a lifeless black world. The fire was over.

# 11 Growing Days

EACH dawn came a little earlier. Each morning the sun seemed a little more eager to fling off his blanket of silver-grey mist, to light with slanting shafts of saffron the ferny hollows and glades beneath the woodland oaks. Each purple twilight came a little later, as the setting sun hung, a red orb poised on the dark shoulder of the moor, and the new grass in the pastures was olive in the fading light.

The travellers were arriving. The yellow wagtail flirted on the sandbar, and waited for the arrival of his mate. The sedge warbler sang in the reed beds by the marsh. The sand martins swooped over the stream, and clung twittering to the steep sandy cliff where the river cut into the field, each year claiming a little more pasture. The swifts arrived in the farmyard, and flew dipping and swooping in and out of the doors of the cowshed. They had travelled thousands of miles, from the dusty heat and the hot white light of the tropics, braving the dangers of the journey and the uncertainty of the English climate, for the benefit of the extra hours of daylight.

In a land where day and night are of equal length, there is not sufficient time for the swifts to gather enough insects to feed their broods. Only the lengthening days of the English spring and summer can give the parent birds the time they need to find the food the growing fledglings need. When the time came, the hen swift would lay three eggs in the nest of mud below the eaves, where the thatch was rotten and honeycombed with holes. The hen laid three eggs, as did her mother and grandmother before her, for to lay more was to invite the death of the brood from starvation. Occasionally a young hen would lay a clutch of four or five eggs. These would hatch, and at first the parent would be equal to the task of raising the young birds. Soon, however, the appetites of the fledglings would outstrip the foraging abilities of the parents, and in their endeavours to share what food there was between all the brood, the parents would starve the lot. So that particular strain would die out, and only the birds which laid three eggs would survive, outnumbering those birds which laid one, or two eggs in a clutch. Thus evolution, the great mathematician, ordained that for swifts, the clutch of eggs should number three.

Each insect-eating bird was similarly controlled, and the great frost, that had killed so many of the insects, had also decimated the bird and bat populations. The insects, being quicker to breed, would replenish their stocks, so that for future generations of birds there would be richer feeding than usual, to help them build up their numbers once more.

From reed bed and sandbar, from copse and thicket, hedgerow and farmyard, the survivors shouted their triumph over the winter and their greeting to the spring. The curlew's call echoed, bubbling and piping, over the tussocky grass of the marshfield, and a blackbird sang by the bridge where the dipper raised a family of young. A thrush called from the topmost branch of the ash, and each morning saw fresh voices to join in the chorus. The tide of spring was in full flood, rushing upwards to high summer, and everywhere was the miracle of new thrusting growth, in a land bursting with secret wealth, the richness of the life force.

Syla drew freely from these coffers of wealth, for the fast-growing embryos in her womb were drawing nourishment from her bloodstream. She showed no sign of the advancing pregnancy. When she stood upright, her slender body was as straight between her flanks as it had ever been. She swam with the same agility, turned just as swiftly, and seemed as tireless as ever. Only her increased appetite, and a growing nervousness of disposition, betrayed her condition.

In the warming, sunlit waters of the river, trout were feeding hungrily on the freely hatching flies. They lay in loose shoals, fanwise at the tail of a stickle, or behind small boulders in the bed of the stream, betraying their presence with the golden flash of their flanks as they turned to intercept the hatching nymphs. The nymphs had spent two long years grubbing and grovelling among the stones and debris at the bottom of the river. Now they were making the fateful journey upwards, at the mercy of wayward current and slashing trout, to break free on the surface of the water. Here they would shed their hard cases of chitin and emerge as adult insects, to dance and mate for a brief while, finally to lay their eggs and die.

Each day Syla took one or two trout. For an hour or two the lie of the trout would remain empty, and then it would be occupied by another. There were always small trout. Only pollution or disease could destroy them absolutely. The law of the wild said that a certain stretch of water could support so many pounds of fish life, but the law paid no heed to the number of units which made up the weight. There could be fifty quarter-pound trout, or twenty-five half-pound trout. The equation was the same.

Syla took trout. She also took eel, loach, bullheads and minnows. There was no way of assessing her predatory ways in terms of good or evil, no writing of a bank balance in black or red ink. She discovered the delights of birds' eggs, and robbed nests indiscriminately as she found them. The bereaved parents moped around the empty nest for a day or so, and then built again. This time the fast-growing foliage hid the nest from Syla, and the second brood was safely reared. Fifty per cent of Syla's diet consisted of fish and eels. Thirty per cent was made up from voles, ten per cent from birds, and the remaining ten per cent consisted of anything from earthworms to frogs and birds' eggs.

She could not have chosen better territory for her survival. The river was small and, in the eyes of man, insignificant. On both sides the steeply wooded cleaves stretched upwards, to lose themselves against the sky in a wilderness of rock and bracken. The trackways through the woods owed their existence mainly to badgers, and so they twisted and wound, here passing beneath a fallen log, here tunnelling straight through a thicket or bramble and thorn. Great granite boulders lay strewn, hidden among the thick undergrowth. By the river the vegetation was almost tropical, growing rank in the steamy heat and dappled light, so that honeysuckle climbed skyward for twenty feet before it opened its perfumed blossoms.

Gradually, as the hill climbed higher, the vegetation passed from sub-tropical to temperate, to a sub-arctic scrub of dwarf birch and mosses, until on the windswept peaks, only the hardiest plants grew, and each plant was specially adapted to survive in waterless conditions of extreme temperature. Here, man was the intruder, and the animals were accustomed to go about their lawful business without reckoning him an enemy. Syla had not seen a man since the half-forgotten day when she was dug out of the rabbit bury. Thus she was taken wholly by surprise when, one day, as she lay sunning herself on a rock in the centre of the stream a man came toiling up the steep and rocky track which followed the river. With the curiosity of her kind she lingered, bright-eyed and alert, watching him as he approached.

The man was small and old, withered and grey like the stunted oaks that surrounded him. His hair and eyebrows were grey, as were his eyes, the only bright thing about him. Weary, and shabbily dressed, a fishing rod in one grey hand, he stood silent now, looking in turn at Syla. She could not know, but she was in no danger from this man. He had spent a lifetime, a long and patient one, asking no more than to be allowed to lose himself in the peace and calm of his own company, to be allowed to watch, to observe, and to wonder. He had had little time for such luxuries. Twice he had served his country in wars which were not of his making. For years he had laboured, in a busy general practice, saving life endangered by folly, struggling to heal people who were sick from their own neglect of themselves, patching worn bodies neglected by their owners. Now he himself was sick, through his own selflessness, and worn out by toil. Now he was too old to enjoy the leisure now granted him. He could only wait to die.

Syla dived from the rock, and for a moment the man thrilled to the sight of her lithe body as it cleaved through the air and hit the water with scarcely a plop. She surfaced a few yards downstream, and the old man watched her head, straining as she paddled towards the far bank. For a moment she posed, dripping wet, on the gravel, before disappearing into the undergrowth. The ferns shook, waved, then all was still.

The old man too stood still, for a long time, and the spring afternoon faded from his sight as his mind drifted back, travelling over years which rang with the din and strife of struggling mankind, until the noise faded away, and Britain lay, a land of bog and forest, of soft marshland and wild moor, a slobbery peninsula, joined to the continent of Europe by a wide land mass which bridged the channel. He saw no men, for as yet they had not begun their triumphal march north-west across Europe. The ice age was receding, although the remains of great glaciers still lay over the mountains of Wales and Scotland, and each winter saw the land buried in deep drifts of snow.

Elk were grazing in the swamps where Charing Cross now stands and beaver built their dams across the river Kennet. Great herds of bison roamed over the plains of Berkshire, and wild boar fought beneath the oaks in the forests of Essex. Over the great undulating Cheshire plain the receding glaciers had laid a fertile bed of deep clayey limy marl, fertilization by a giant and prolific hand, which was to provide rich grazing for centuries to come, and which, in the deeper hollows, had left sparkling meres of alkaline water which were to become rich with teeming aquatic life.

A small cloud passed over the sun; the old man shivered, opening his eyes once more on the present. For a brief moment Syla had shown him a glimpse of the greatness that once had been, for the sight of her, alien in a land which thousands of years ago had been her rightful heritage, had reminded him of those days, and had jolted him into realizing just how wantonly the riches of the land, bestowed on him by natural forces long since expired, had been squandered by man, the thinker. Regretfully, he tied a light olive to the gossamer nylon of his cast, his old eyes squinting against the light and as he began to cast, he meditated a trifle ruefully, wondering what the face of the countryside would now be like, had we known at the beginning what we know now; had we spent our wealth wisely, instead of squandering it; conserved our heritage, instead of exploiting it.

A small trout took his fly, and came twisting in a series

of gold flashes to the bank, where the old man bent down. Taking hold of the hook, he released the little fish, allowing it to shake itself free without touching it with his fingers. It darted away into the depths, and the old man dried his fly, lengthening his line before casting again into the black run of water under the far bank. The surface of the water bulged momentarily, and the split-cane rod bent as the trout ran upriver. The old man played it casually, almost absent-mindedly, his mind still musing on what might have been. The trout turned, and lay on its side, resigned to its fate as the old man drew it towards the net. He shook himself as he drew the fish over the net. He was an old man, a failure in the eyes of many, he knew little of economics, the balance of power, of trends, of politics. Again he released the trout, this time nursing it until it regained its strength and equilibrium, and was able to swim away on an even keel. He had seen enough of death in his time.

The old man moved away upriver, and even his passing, gentle and inconspicuous as it was, left small waves of consequence, ripples of cause and effect. A jay screamed a warning as it marked his passage, a squirrel raced away through the tree tops at the sound. The squirrel alarmed a flock of bluetits that fed among the branches of a rowan, and as they fled a sparrowhawk scythed through their ranks, picking out a hen bird in a small explosion of golden feathers. This spared the life of a cock chaffinch that was already being pursued by the hawk. For three more days the chaffinch lived to sing his repetitive song of joy, until at dawn he was fascinated, along with a score of other small birds, by the antics of a weasel with a leaf. He sat huddled on the ground, watching as the weasel twisted and turned, leapt and danced, until animal and leaf were a blur of chestnut. Then dawn ended in a mist of red as the weasel closed its teeth on his throat.

Syla slept for an hour after the man had gone, to awake, hungry, as the first chill of evening swept through the wood. As the old man drove his little car slowly back to his bungalow, she slipped into the river where he had first surprised her, and worked her way steadily up the deep dark run under the bank. Here she came upon a trout, more than eight ounces in weight, which swam with a strange lethargy, and which died with scarcely a struggle. Syla, frustrated at the lack of a chase, released it and caught it again several times before she ended its life. She did not see, or paid no heed, to the small wound in its jaw, where an hour before a hook had held the fish captive.

# 12 Fulfilment

THE sun shone, and the wind blew soft, shaking the catkins so that they showered their golden dust on the female flowers below them. Warm rain fell in shining silver sheets, polishing the rocks, swelling the river, plumping the soil so that countless million rootlets absorbed moisture, carrying it up a million green stems, so that trillions of green leaves could transpire it back into the atmosphere. With the coming of the night, the sun-warmed, moistened air cooled, and gave back the moisture as dew. Once more it began its journey, into the soil, through the roots, up the stems, and out through the leaves into the sunlit air. Millions and untold millions of gallons of water travelled thus each day, and played a small part in the pattern of the growing year.

The water that travelled through the oak nourished the leaves, and the leaves nourished a host of caterpillars that fed upon them. Bluetits came and fed upon the caterpillars, and the strength of the caterpillars' grip on the oak twig was so strong that as the bluetit pulled the grub, the tough outer skin of the grub tore. This made the grub fit for digestion by the young bluetit, and saved the parent bird from the task of dismembering the grub. The numbers of young bluetits had already been ordained some weeks before, by the same climatic conditions that ordained the numbers of the grubs, so that there was no chance of the young bluetits running short of food. Always there would be sufficient, always the bluetits would survive, always some grubs would reach maturity to perpetuate their race, and always the oaks would survive, to feed future generations of grubs and birds.

The moisture evaporating from the leaves and grasses kept the land cool. Without it, and without the impounding of the water in the untold millions of tiny green reservoirs, which released their store of moisture slowly and frugally, the rising sun would dry the dew in an instant, and the bare surface of the land would immediately grow unbearably hot. The reptiles knew this, the grass snake and the adder, the slow worm, the sand lizard, the common lizard, and the rare smooth snake, all sought the hot bareness of rock and sand, which warmed quickly in the sun's rays, and which were miniature deserts, hot in contrast to the green ocean around them. The reptiles were cold-blooded, and took for themselves the temperature of the land around them, but they knew how to regulate this body temperature within the necessary limits, by seeking the environment with the temperature nearest to the optimum.

The moisture which kept the land cool during the hours of sunlight, also kept the earth warm at night. Water cools more slowly than sand or rock, and without its burden of sun-warmed moisture, the earth at night would lose its heat so rapidly that temperatures would drop below freezing, long before another dawn. Water was the life-giver, and each living thing was adapted to acquire a sufficiency of water, and to conserve it without waste. The fish spent its entire life in water. The frog, which lost water through its skin, carried a reservoir of water as an emergency supply. The reptile wore a waterproof skin. The mammals drank, filtered their body moisture through their kidneys, and cautiously voided small amounts only to rid themselves of impurities. Many had adapted themselves to manage with less and less moisture, and some of the rodents spent all their lives without taking a single drink. They gained enough moisture from the food they ate.

The predators drank most of all, for they lived on a diet rich in proteins and salts, which formed excesses in their bloodstream, which had to be voided lest they proved toxic. Even so, they conserved moisture by controlling their metabolism to such a degree that they did not need to perspire to keep cool. This they managed by staying small, so that the heat loss from their body was fairly rapid. To prevent it becoming too rapid in winter they grew a thicker coat, which by the coming of the summer proved too effective.

With the coming of May Syla began to shed her winter coat, and to emerge smart and sleek in a shorter, glossier pelt. At the same time she went more frequently to the hollow log, and during the short nights she spent many hours scratching and burrowing in one corner, until she had scooped out quite a respectable hollow in the rotten wood. Here she brought dried grass and fern, finely shredded twigs and moss, birch bark, pine needles, stray feathers, and a paper handkerchief tissue that she had found by the river. These she tore and combed into a finely woven nest, and here she shed a great deal of her winter coat, as she burrowed and bored in her efforts at nest making. Twice she turned the whole lot out and started again, dissatisfied with her efforts, and each time she collected fresh bedding, to which she added the old, until in time the whole log was packed with dry, dead vegetation.

Here too she brought her playthings, the skull of the weasel that had lain in the log when she first found it, a horse's tooth, yellow and worn, which she had found by the river, a small pebble white and round, which normally she kept at the bottom of a pool, knowing always where to find it. These, together with the mummified foot of a heron, seemed suddenly to become more and more important to her. She began to sleep in the log, at first intermittently, and on rare occasions, then with ever-growing frequency, until after a week she was spending every day there. When she slept she gathered her possessions around her, and seemed to find comfort from the pressure of them against her chest and abdomen. Always she dried herself with meticulous care, and the final effort of pushing herself through the long tunnel of bedding rendered her short pelt bone dry by the time she reached the bed chamber.

For several days no rain had fallen, and the sun shone with fierce intensity out of a cloudless sky. From early dawn the cuckoo called incessantly, and with the coming of the dusk the nightjar flitted ghostlike along the river, his churring call mingling with the sleepy chink of tired blackbirds, and the thin evensong of the robin. The nightjar was a bird of unusual habits, which had earned him a bad name with superstitious humans. The nightjar sought insects on the wing, and at night he would haunt the pastures where sheep and cattle grazed, flickering and diving round them as he snapped up insects disturbed by the grazing animals. Humans thought he sucked the milk of the beasts, and called him 'goatsucker'. He would follow humans as they walked in the dark, for the same reason, that their clumsy feet, hot bodies, and glimmering lanterns, disturbed hosts of insects. The humans, frightened and perplexed by the wheeling, ghost-like shape that followed them, labelled him 'corpsehound', and said he was the soul of an unbaptized baby, come to haunt them. He was but a bird, and his miracle was of life, not death.

In the heat and yellow glare of the days insects thrived and prospered, dancing above the black water of the river as the cool dusk stole hand in hand with the night. Then the bats, the fortunate ones which had survived the winter by the kinder environment of the stream, wheeled and dipped through the dark caverns of the oaks. Within a few hours daylight came again, and the predators returned to their lairs, full fed quickly, for such was the surplus of easy prey. Then the heat came again, and the hen birds panted as they brooded their young, sheltering them with their wings from the fierce heat.

The river ran clear and low, the bleached bones of the boulders showing above the surface. The leaves of the plants drooped in the heat, and growth slowed down, awaiting the coming of the rain. Meanwhile, the plants pushed their roots deeper into the soil, and millions more root hairlets formed, extracting all available moisture from the soil. By the middle of the month the river had dropped a foot, and several small springs had dried up completely.

Another day dawned, without any dew, for the night had been as sultry as the preceding day. By lunchtime, the sun was hidden behind a veil of sulphurous yellow, and the trees hung silent and expectant in a windless sky. The light shone with a strange unearthly intensity, and the hot dry air seemed to crackle in its dryness. No bird sang, even the cuckoo was silent. No leaf stirred, no nodding fern or trembling grass betrayed the movement of animal life. Only the incessant buzz of countless small black flies broke the silence of the waiting world.

The yellow tint of the sky deepened, until by mid-afternoon the sun shone like polished brass from an angry, copper-hued sky, a sky which tinged to deepest purple over the far-distant hills.

Suddenly, it was as if the earth sighed, and a faint breeze lifted the leaves of the oaks, turning them in disarray and showing their undersides. The breeze drifted by, seemed to fade in abortive death, then all at once it swelled, growing with obscene force into a roaring, soughing wind, and at its command, as if they had been lying in ambush below the curve of the distant moors, small clouds appeared from all parts of the compass. Swiftly they travelled across the glowering sky, growing rapidly in stature as they converged in silence over the waiting cleave, great grey veils, their undersides heavy with moisture, hanging in pendulant curves, the dreaded cumulus mammatus.

Now the sky was black with their presence, and it seemed as if premature night had descended upon the wood. In tree and bush, in rock crevice and hollow stump, in the clinging protection of the ivy, and under dense canopy of leaf, the birds settled to sleep, for there was nothing else they could do. The lizard slid away under the stones, the adder crawled down a mouse hole, the fish lay inert on the bed of the stream. Together, each and every animal bowed its head and awaited the coming of the storm.

White light split the blackness in a flickering forking rent, starting the wild life awake in time to hear the answering crash and roll of the thunder that followed. The initial flash was followed instantly by another, crackling and spiteful, and again the hills echoed and re-echoed with the pent-up fury of the storm. Then the rain came, spattering down star shells on the soft grey dust, and whipping the surface of the river to a white and foaming sea of froth. The smell of wet granite was strong in the air, and the leaves and plants bowed as the delicate inter-tracery of twig and leaf was shattered and destroyed by the force of the water.

The ash tree where the thrush sang each day was split asunder, riven and smoking by the searing blast of a purple lightning streak. One great branch lay broken on the ground, and the riven trunk, split lengthways for twelve feet, bled the life sap of the tree away. Scattered over the turf lay the bodies of three fledgling woodpeckers, and a grey squirrel, which had sheltered in one of the many hollows, fled for cover.

After the rain came hail, ice-sharp and heavy, cutting further into the green blanket of leaf and grass. The fells ran with brown, peat-stained water, and the agitated trout moved restlessly as the waters of the river quickened and discoloured. Cautiously they sought the shelter of quieter waters near the banks, and then, as the swirling current began to carry down its debris of leaf and twig, they began to feed on the multitude of worms, grubs and insects that had been swept into the river by the storm and drowned. For several hours they gorged, until at length the river ran bank-high, sour and choked with silt, and then the trout once more lay dormant in the eddies and slacks, away from the main force of the current. The water was warm and stale. The trout felt sickened and their gills worked rapidly as they struggled to gain sufficient oxygen from the turbid water.

Long into the night the storm raged, and any animal who had not been circumspect enough to find secure shelter died from the fury of its blows. Corpses drifted downstream: a magpie, a nest of fieldmice, a lamb, a litter of newborn rabbits. Many fledglings drifted downstream, their sightless eyes staring and their voiceless beaks agape. Trout ate a few. The rest would be found, and eaten later, by the herons, crows and rats. Nothing would be wasted. No life would be spent in vain.

Slowly the storm moved away. The intervals between the flashes of lightning grew longer, and the voice of the thunder less loud. For several hours the rain fell steadily, the distant hills flickered with light, and the thunder muttered low across the dark and soggy land. Then the rain ceased, and a star shone in each puddle and rain drop. A thin crescent moon looked down on the ravished land, and white clouds, sped by a fresh cool breeze, swept across a violet sky.

Alone in the log, Syla lay panting, overcome with heat and fear. Outside she could hear the storm raging, and the drumming of the hail on the outside of the log almost drove her into bolting out into the open. A strange lethargy made her lie still, and from time to time her breathing quickened. Then she half rose, to collapse again, her flanks heaving, her body tumultuous with strange gripping pains. Panic-stricken, she clung to her playthings, and found consolation in their familiar hard feel. At last she heard the passing of the storm, and for a moment she ventured out into the clear cold night. She drank, quenching her thirst in the nearest rain puddle, and then slipped back into the warmth and security of her lair. The fulfilment of her life had come, and with the age old wisdom of instinct, Syla knew exactly what was expected of her.

# 13 The Family

DURING the remaining three hours of darkness, Syla gave birth to five kitts. Earlier in her pregnancy she had lost a sixth, without being aware of the fact. The fertilized egg had drifted free from its insecure attachment to her womb, and whilst still minute and undeveloped, had been washed away unnoticed.

As each kitt arrived, Syla severed the umbilical cord with her teeth and ate the placenta, fastidiously clearing away every scrap of debris. Then she washed and dried the kitt, massaging life into it until it pushed and squirmed against the warmth of her flank. The last to arrive was a female, weak and puny, without the strength to suck. Unknown to Syla, it had a cleft palate, and for two days its feeble and plaintive mewing upset Syla, agitating her so that she could not settle comfortably to feed her kitts. On the third night its cries weakened and died, so that Syla forgot it and lay on it. Soon it was lost in the deep litter of the nest, and its body dried and mummified.

Of the remaining four kitts, two were males, and two females. Each was naked, hairless and blind, about the length of a cigarette, and very little thicker. During the first twenty-four hours of their existence, Syla left them only for a few moments, once to drink, after she had awakened from the sleep of after-birth exhaustion, and once to deposit a small, black, tarry dropping, which was all that remained of the five placentae. The remainder of the time she spent dozing, washing the kitts, and in quiet enjoyment of the sensual pleasure their heaving bodies gave to her flanks.

At first she was alert to clear away every tiny spot of excrement, and as each kitt produced its minute dropping, or dew drops of urine, Syla cleared it away. After about a week, she was to tire of the ever increasing chore, and then she would deposit each kitt in turn, after it had fed, in a certain part of the nest. After it had produced its offerings, she would allow it to return to her side, and so, before their eyes were open, the kitts learnt the lesson of cleanliness. Syla the houseproud would then take the soiled bedding and carry it some distance from the log, before dropping it and returning with a clean supply.

During the first week Syla's hunting forays were brief and savage. She killed quickly, ate what she needed, and then hurried back to the nest. If she fished, she was careful to dry herself before she re-entered the nest. The kitts grew fast, rapidly acquiring sleek coats of fine hair, and one female, Salla, was a pale fawn in colour. She carried the prized strain of pastel blood from some ancestor.

The days were warm and fine again, and the temperature in the log grew hot, the air stuffy. Syla spread the bedding flat and lay apart from the kitts, which sprawled in sleepy abandon on the soft litter. Already the two males, Kiva and Bara, were lustier than the females, but Syla had plenty of rich milk with which to nourish all four. The kitts fed about six times a day, and Syla drank more than she had ever done before.

One hot afternoon, as the kitts lay feeding, Syla was startled by a loud knock on the log. She was on her feet in an instant, scattering her kitts about the nest, and next moment she was racing down the log, to peer out of a small hole and scream anger and defiance at the disturber of the peace. The knocker was Hekel the green woodpecker, hunting for grubs. So terrified was this worthy at the apparition that had answered his summons that he somersaulted backwards off the log, and lay flat on his back, screaming in abject misery, while his four-clawed feet beat the empty air. Syla surveyed him for a moment with tolerant contempt, then returned to her babies, while Hekel flew shakily away, not quite sure that he really had seen what he had seen.

Kiva's eyes opened on the tenth day, and the others opened theirs on the eleventh and twelfth days. Still they could not see, and there was no light in the log, but immediately they grew more active, tottering to and fro in the nest and jostling each other. Their bodies were short and fat, their legs long and straight. Their heads seemed too big for their bodies. From the moment they were born the kitts exercised, and even when they were feeding, their hind legs, pushing and straining as they nuzzled into their mother's side, were being developed so that the muscles would grow firm and strong. Now they progressed from crawling to standing upright, tottering and shaky. Each time one kitt knocked another over, the muscles of the fallen kitt were brought into play in the effort of heaving upright. By the time the kitts were three weeks old they were quite active and sturdy, moving surely in the darkness of the log and harmlessly worrying each other with their sharp white little teeth.

These teeth, and the sharp little claws which the kitts wore, were beginning to worry Syla. She was glad to escape for a while to be alone in the warmth and security of the short summer night, and to lie in the stream, feeling the soothing lap of the cool water against her scratched and fevered skin. As the heat of the day passed and the leather-winged bats emerged to hunt in the twilight, Syla would slip out from the log, drink her fill by the river, and then enjoy the luxury of a bathe. Refreshed, she would make her way upstream, hunting for trout and eels, until, after an hour or so, she would return overland, to check on her kitts and satisfy herself that all was well. Then she would leave them again until dawn, returning as the trunks of the oaks emerged strong and black from the darkness.

One morning she killed a wood vole as she returned to the nest. She had no hunger, having fed well, but instead of leaving the limp warm corpse she picked it up and carried it with her, her cheeks and whiskers bloody with her prize, taking it into the nest. Here she tore it to shreds, dropping small morsels of shredded flesh, heart, and liver, in front of the kitts. The kitts, all but one, fell on the tiny morsels with clumsy greed, mumbling and mouthing them, wasting more than they ate. One female refused to have anything to do with the meat. This was Salla, the pastel, the smallest of the four.

Syla fed all four kitts with her milk, and cleared up the gory remains that littered the nest. Next night, as soon as she had quenched her thirst, Syla caught a small trout, and took it straight back to the nest. This time Salla fed as greedily as the others, and there was very little left of the trout when they had finished. Kiva ate most, and Syla left him and Bara playing tug of war with the head. At dawn Syla brought a fledgling thrush, but the kitts found this difficult to manage. They choked and sneezed over the feathers, and played with more than they ate. Still, they were learning all the time. Their jaws were growing stronger, and the tug of war games were splendid exercise for the little mink.

On a warm moonless night in June, as a soft wind blew clouds from the west, Syla, in a state of high nervous tension, led her kitts out from the log. For several nights Kiva and Bara had tried to follow her when she had left the nest, and she had had to drive them back with cuffs and snarls. Now, at her bidding, the kitts tumbled eagerly out of the log, the two males leading, then Salla, finally the other female, Jeta. Jeta was very small and slim, yet she was perhaps the most active and wiry of the four.

Once in the open, the kitts hesitated, peering myopically into a darkness that was yet lighter than the midday gloom of the log. Syla lay at the entrance to the log, watching the kitts as they explored the vastness of the open air with short nervous rushes. Rather lost and bewildered, the kitts wandered around, sniffing at the variety of plants that grew in the little clearing, and soon a game of tag developed, as Kiva hid behind a fern, and rushed out at Bara as he passed.

The playground of the kitts was formed from the hollow at the end of the log. This hollow had been created as the tree fell, tearing with it its roots. Here vegetation was sparse, and the steep sides of the hollow made an effective barrier, preventing the kitts from straying far. The climb upwards was too much for their shaky little legs, and inevitably they tired, lost their grip, overbalanced and rolled to the bottom of the hollow. Once again, however, it was good exercise.

Twenty minutes of vigilance was as much as Syla's nerves could stand on this first night, and soon she was bundling a protesting quartet back into the log. The activity and adventure had exhausted them, and soon they were sound asleep. They awoke once during the night, when Syla brought them a trout, and then again at dawn. This time Syla had an eel and they crunched happily at the white, meaty flesh, getting well and truly slimy in the process. For the first time, the little kitts made some attempt at a toilet, and later Syla cleaned up the spots they had missed.

From that night, the kitts played outside regularly. The weather remained warm and fine, with no dew, and when Syla returned with food she would call them out, depositing the prize at their feet. Still she dismembered the catch for them, and still she supplemented their rations with her milk. Each night saw the kitts grow a little sturdier, a little more independent, a bit more active, and soon the time would come when Syla would be able to lead them on their first foray, away from the nest. Meanwhile they played in the hollow, although they could now scale the sides, and spring down on each other from the top.

Sometimes Syla romped with them, wrestling and rolling in mock combat. The play was tuition for the stern life that was to follow. The tug of war with a bird's wing, when the kitt hung on with eyes tight shut, growling fiercely and backing away all the while, was to become the terrible bite of death, eyes closed against injury, whilst dragging the opponent along so as to throw him off balance and hinder his strike. In the hollow the kitts learnt all the rudiments of hunting and killing: the stalk, the pounce, the bite, always on head, neck or throat. They learnt how to use their weight, throwing it on to one shoulder as they darted in to the 'kill', so as to throw the opponent and expose its vulnerable underparts to needle-clawed, raking hind legs.

Syla watched proudly as her sons grew in strength and vigour, and many other eyes watched the kitts at play. Hoo the tawny owl watched from the oak, his great amber eyes wide and his large ears listening. Convulsively, his claws gripped the rough bark of the branch as he slowly turned his old head, but always he refrained from attacking. A fox passed by, and stood poised in a thicket of fern, one paw delicately upraised. With the silence that only a fox can command, he moved in for a closer look, but when he saw Syla he retreated with equal caution. Syla's reputation was now well known among her fellow predators.

Once a family of badgers blundered down to the hollow, and the kitts fled pell-mell for the safety of the log. Syla stood her ground, and gave one sharp scream. Instantly the great blundering beasts stopped their crashing and stood frozen, black and white faces poised, statuesque in the undergrowth. Then with a snort of exasperation the old boar turned away, his feet thudding on the hard earth. The family followed, and soon the noise of their passage died away in the wood.

Death watched too, staring with hard glittering eyes which never closed. Death lay coiled in the tangled roots of a thorn bush, and one night Salla ran fearlessly to meet her fate. She saw the adder, which never moved, and Salla moved closer, curious, and eager to try out some of the lessons she had learnt in her games. She was a little way away from the other kitts, but she could hear them playing, and her mother was resting in the hollow. She felt herself to be in no danger, and the adder's pointed tail lay within easy reach. The tail moved a fraction, and Salla struck, biting hard, and backing away with her eyes closed. The reptile was in no way embarrassed by this manoeuvre, and Salla felt the slight blow of his strike, the needle sharpness of his teeth, as they sank into her neck, and the spread of liquid fire as the poison seeped into her body.

Her teeth clenched harder in her agony, then her jaws opened wide and her body arched as she screamed in death. By the time Syla reached her side her body was already relaxing, and lay limp, without a tremor. The adder had gone, fading away into the night to nurse his injured tail and await the renewal of his venom.

Syla picked up the body of Salla and trotted to and from the nest several times in the anguish of indecision. Finally, at the spot near to where Salla was killed, she dropped the body, licked it several times, and then returned to her remaining kitts. She drove them back into the log, and went away to the river. By morning she had killed and eaten twice, and when she returned to the hollow with meat for her kitts, she had forgotten all about Salla.

The dead kitt did not lie long above the soil. A vespillo burying beetle found it while it was still warm, and after crawling over it the grave beetle solemnly moved to a spot a little way away, where the earth was soft and moist. He began to dig, and very soon he had excavated a hollow very much the size of Salla. Then he returned to the corpse, and using his legs as levers, he pushed from underneath, moving Salla nearer and nearer her grave. Soon he was joined by a second beetle, and under their joint efforts, Salla moved more quickly.

At last she lay at rest, and the two beetles dug down beneath her again, so that she sank still lower into the soil. The loose earth thrown up by the beetles soon covered her, but the beetles remained underground. When they emerged, the female would have laid her eggs in the body of Salla, and there her grubs would feed until they reached maturity.

# 14 Voyagers of the Rain

THE long fine spell, which had been broken only by the storm, dissolved into smoking white wreaths of cloud, and a fine rain shimmered and danced over the parched moors, polishing the lichen-stained granite, and adorning each blade of grass, each nodding frond of fern, with a thousand sparkling diamond drops. It darkened the pendulous leaves, and plumped the dusty earth, bestowing a gentle beneficence that was without hurt to any living creature. The river rose slowly, and ran high and clear, free from all impurity, and effervescent with sparkling, life-giving oxygen. The weight of its current pushed a long, questing finger of fresh water far out beyond the estuary, into the blue salt waters of the bay, and it carried a message for the voyagers of the rain.

They had been waiting, the sea trout, since early spring, shoaling in deep rocky chasms where the sea floor was white sand, and the brown kelp waved its long banners in the restless tide. They had lain on sandbars rich with feed of silt, where launce lay buried, sheltered from packs of feeding turbot, which browsed like cattle in the shallow brown waters. The seatrout had evaded the marauding gangs of killer bass, which struck like wolves swooping down from the sunlight waters of the surface, and which could engulf a small sea trout with one chop of their capacious maws. To and fro they had travelled with the tide, running the gauntlet of porpoise and heron, otter and lamprey, bass and tope, and their numbers were so great that the inroads carved by the predators made no noticeable gap in their ranks.

With the sea trout came salmon, and at low tide both salmon and sea trout faced a fresh hazard, for across the narrow gut of the estuary fishermen laid nets, and swept the sea in great half circles, trapping the fish and hauling them landward. For a brief moment their bodies thrashed in the entwining mesh of the net. Then they danced a frenzied tattoo of death on gravel bar, or deck of boat, before being hit on the head and sold to hotels. Now the regiments felt the pull of the river, strong and clear, and they surged forward with powerful thrust of body and tail, obedient to the call which they and their ancestors had obeyed for millions of years. They made for the hills, where the streams were small and the water pure, where gravel lay unburdened with silt, and where they could lay their eggs in water cold enough to be free of disease, pure enough for the delicate alevins, sheltered enough for the tiny parr to survive.

By night they journeyed, under bridges over which diesel trains clattered and thundered, past lamp-lit cottages where unseeing humans lived, loved, hated and died, between lush meadows where fat red cattle browsed, or lay chewing the cud. Some went on up the main river, over weirs and through wide parklands, where fallow deer grazed among the spreading oaks, but others turned off, up the lesser tributary, towards the cleave and the woodland where Syla had her kitts. Their journey was secret. The running fox and the mousing owl hunted in the undergrowth on both sides of the stream, but they knew nothing of the voyagers. The otter knew, and the heron. The bailiff saw them, like symbols of ancient heraldry, their serried ranks black against a backcloth of golden gravel, as they rested in the pools by day, and the poachers saw them, but pretended not to, as they went to work in the grey light of the misty morning. Now the voyagers were more vulnerable than they had ever been before.

The bigger sea trout came first, hen fish up to ten or twelve pounds in weight, but most of them around three or four pounds apiece. Perhaps they were anxious to be first on the gravel redds, and were prepared to endure the long wait for the privilege of securing the best spawning sites, or perhaps they had merely had their fill of ocean feeding. The shoals of smaller summer peal were to come later, fish between twelve and twenty-four ounces in weight. They perhaps lingered because they wanted to make the most of the rich harvest of the sea.

The first sea trout to complete the arduous journey through the jagged rocks and foaming white water that raced down the cleave was a hen sea trout of three-and-a-half pounds. She made the journey so fast that she arrived in the quiet water of the salmon pool still silver, with her gills crusted with sea lice. On this night Syla took her kitts to the water for the first time.

By now Kiva and Bara were almost as big as she was. Only Jeta betrayed her sex by her smaller size. All three followed their mother solemnly, and with exaggerated caution, overawed and impressed with the strangeness of the world around them. The kitts paused on the gravel spit, disliking the cold harsh feel of the grit between their claws, and thrust inquiring noses into the black, oil liquid that flowed silently by. Sneezing and spluttering they drew back, whimpering with dismay as they saw their mother slide into the water, calling over her shoulder as she swam. Kiva followed almost immediately, feeling first a sudden wave of fear and panic, to be followed by elation and wonder as he felt the new element bear him up and carry him along. Automatically his legs kicked out and thrust him through the water, and though his efforts were clumsy compared with his mother's grace and style, he strove manfully to emulate her.

After a moment's hesitation Bara followed, rather more splashily, and with much spluttering and squeaking protest. He too discovered the delights of the water, and soon the two brothers were spashing together in the shallows, endeavouring to catch each other's tail. Jeta stayed on the gravel spit, whimpering and backing away whenever one of the trio approached her, and after a while Syla swam away, leaving the male kitts playing and Jeta whimpering, to fish along a narrow black run that was created by two boulders in the bed of the stream. As she swam, intent on the dark silhouette of a small trout in front of her, she was momentarily disturbed by a great silver flash on her right, and a sudden turbulence in the water. She returned to the pursuit of the small trout, and killed it as it drove towards a shallow slack. Then she returned to the kitts, but the memory of the underwater encounter returned and excited her curiosity.

Shouldering off the vociferous attentions of the males, Syla landed on the gravel spit and dropped the trout in front of Jeta. Eagerly the hungry kitt ran forward, but Syla snatched up the trout and retreated into the water with it, holding it loosely in her jaws, and calling Jeta to come. Jeta retreated once more, growling and whimpering, so Syla swam back to the shore, dropping the fish in the water, just beyond Jeta's reach.

Jeta moved forward cautiously, reaching far out for the prize, but the little trout drifted slowly away, and Jeta retreated once more. Kiva darted past his mother and snapped up the trout, while Bara seized the tail of the fish and tried to wrest it from Kiva.

By now thoroughly exasperated with her wayward daughter, Syla marched out of the water and on to the spit. Roughly she seized Jeta by the scruff of her neck and dragged the protesting, squirming mink into the river. Here she towed Jeta far out into mid-stream, and then let her go. Jeta sank, and water choked her cries, scalding her nose and throat. Frantically she fought, and her kicks brought her to the surface, where, like her brothers, she found she could swim. As she made for the bank her fears gradually departed, and, spying her brothers still squabbling over the trout, she turned to join them.

The trout, in three pieces, was carried by the kitts to the gravel bar, and by the time they had finished it and combed the ground for scales, Syla was waiting at the water's edge with an eel. This she chopped up, allowing the fragments to drift away, slowly sinking in the stream, and now the kitts not only had to swim for their supper, but dive for it as well. All three kitts managed to retrieve a piece, but most of the eel was lost downstream. At length, Syla led them back to the nest, showing them how to dry themselves by rolling and twisting in the dry grass and ferns near the log.

The kitts had one more duty to perform, and each in turn went to a toilet area near the log, to deposit its droppings on the pile already accumulated there. This pile had grown like an odoriferous stalagmite, so that each kitt had to perform a feat of acrobatics to deposit its offering near the top. From henceforth this pile was to be abandoned, and a fresh one formed near the river.

For generations mink, and other members of the weasel tribe had performed this rite as the better of two alternatives. The mound of droppings, in such close proximity to the nest, was conspicuous, if it was found. Even so, it was less evident than numerous small droppings scattered over a wide area of countryside, and thus it was less likely to be noticed. Only man was likely to interpret the pile as evidence of a family close by, and he was ever unobservant about such matters. As a predator, the mink was less worried about betraying her presence to enemies, than frightening away her prey. Most predators had some trick with which to maintain their anonymity. The badger had his latrines, with their little pits dug in the soft soil. The owl had a favourite perch, where he digested his meals, and the ground below the perch was littered with regurgitated castings of fur and beetle shards.

By much the same apparent paradox, a shoal of fish

offered its members immunity from attack. A predator finding such a shoal could wreak havoc in a short space of time, but a predator could search a long time before locating such a shoal, whereas if fish were scattered uniformly over the river, it would be impossible to find a square yard not tenanted by at least one individual.

With the kitts at rest, Syla remembered the strange encounter in the salmon pool, and returned to the river. So far she had not fed that night, and with her hunger her hunting instincts became paramount. Swiftly, she made her way over the short rocky path, through the twisted spiny stems of the trailing bramble. All around her the woodland breathed perceptibly in the dim light of the stars. Quiet rustlings and squeaks emitted from shadow and brake. White moths fluttered among the alders, and an owl hooted softly in the far distance. A hedgehog blundered along, snorting and snuffling as it searched for crane flies in the long grass of the clearing. Syla ignored it, for the sound of the river was loud in her ears.

At the gravel spit she paused, one paw upraised, watching and listening as the quiet water flowed past. In the stillness, above the distant roar of the white water, she heard a click, a tiny sound suspended in the darkness somewhere between sky and earth. Tense with apprehension, Syla waited.

It came again, clearly audible on the night air, a tiny clatter as if a stone had been turned, somewhere up river where the water foamed down from the steps. It was still some distance away, and came no nearer. Syla ignored it and slid silently into the pool.

The sea trout lay in deep water on the opposite bank,

under the overhanging branches of an alder, where a white gob of foam eddied and swirled in slow, endless circles. She felt the soft intrusion of Syla's body as the mink entered the water, the radiating waves pulsing slowly along her lateral line, and the fish sank down, pressing her body to the yielding gravel, and waiting with fins and tail curled, ready for immediate flight. The waves of turbulence grew firmer and stronger, as Syla swam towards her, twisting this way and that in an endeavour to locate the fish.

Motionless, the sea trout was invisible to Syla. Not until she moved would she betray her presence with a flash of silver flank. Now there was to follow a war of nerves, as Syla quested blindly to and fro, quartering the dark waters, and gradually, unwittingly, drawing nearer to the fish. Once Syla surfaced to draw air, passing over the fish as she turned and swam down the pool.

The sea trout stirred, and Syla spotted the slight movement, thrust towards it with frantic kicks of her powerful hind legs. The sea trout waited until Syla's face, silvered with tiny air bubbles trapped among the fur, was within a foot of her. Then she surged forward with all the power of her muscular flanks, hitting Syla on the shoulder and knocking her over and over with the force of the blow, and further adding to her discomfort with a stunning blow of her tail. Furious, Syla went in pursuit, this time more wary of her prey, hounding the fish up and down the narrow confines of the pool, striving to drive the fish into the shallows beyond.

At length the mink was forced to surface again, to draw air and dog paddle on the surface. At this moment a heavy splash upstream attracted her attention, and she saw, in the split second before she dived again, three black forms, all vastly bigger than herself, and one twice the size of the other two, swimming towards her. The sea trout forgotten, Syla swam underwater for the far bank, and the sloping rock at the tail of the pool. Hastily she scrambled out, shook herself, and vanished into the undergrowth. Then, feeling more secure, her curiosity overcame her fear, and she made her way cautiously back to the river bank, watching from the shelter of a blackthorn thicket.

The bitch otter swam unhurriedly down the pool, keeping close under the opposite bank, and leaving her cubs at the head of the pool. In the shallow water near the weir the bitch dived, her vast bulk creating a turbulence in which the paling stars, for it was now near dawn, flickered and danced with her passing. Now thoroughly alarmed, and still unfamiliar with the topography of the pool, the sea trout sped away, only to meet the waiting jaws of the cubs. Frantically it turned, cutting back down the pool, with the cubs following, but less than half way down she met the bitch. The black shelter of an overhanging rock lay to her left, and the fish shot under it, jarring her back and spine as she came violently against the shelf of rock.

There she lay, fearful, as the three otters nosed slowly along the narrow cleft, strings of bubbles rising from their questing muzzles. Fear robbed the sea trout of confidence in the safety of her retreat, and in desperation she shot out again, darting between the cubs and buffeting them with the waves of her flight. The bitch, anticipating this move, closed on her with open jaws. The white teeth clashed, crushing down through scale and creamy flesh, shattering spine and nerves.

Triumphant, the otters dragged their prey to the gravel spit, while Syla bickered and danced with impotent rage, and for a moment considered attacking the poachers who had robbed her of her prize. Prudence, fortunately, prevailed; a very savage mink went hunting for voles along thc river bank. Vcry latc she returned to the nest, as the sun was already breaking over the hill, but she was full fed, and in a better temper, as she called the kitts out to breakfast on a great mouthful of tiny pink fieldmice.

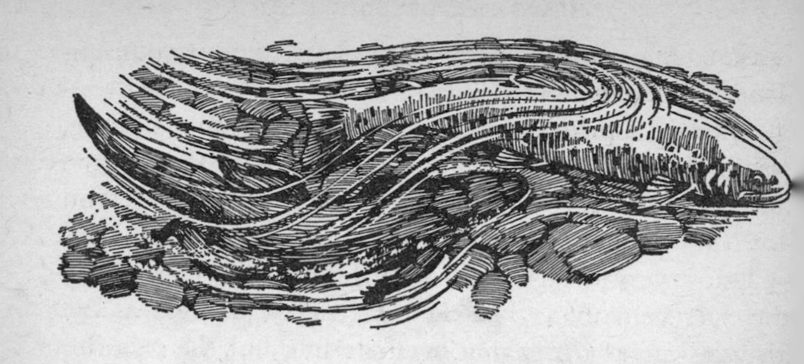

# 15 The Full of the Tide

THE tide of summer was in full flood, and hung slack, waiting for the run off. Under the full-leafed oaks the vegetation was rank and long, exhausted with its struggle for light and supremacy. On the hill bracken stood as high as a man, and fox and badger wandered abroad in full daylight, concealed even from the eyes of Arak, the raven, the all-seeing.

Meadowsweet foamed white along the river bank, and tall thickets of balsam, the invader, barred the way with their fragrant leaves. The warm air was fragrant with a thousand scents, as myriads of plants flaunted their charms in the hope of a ravishing caress from bee or butterfly. The lizard crouched beside her pocket of eggs and at night the glow worms shone, pale green sapphires of light amid the grass stems. Birds sat silent in wood and copse, with tattered wings and balding pates, suffering from the strange lethargy which overwhelmed them partly due to the strain and hard work of rearing their young, and partly because of the nearness of the moulting season. The cuckoos had gone, back to the hot bright lands from whence they came, and soon the chestnut-feathered offspring, so unlike the parent it had never seen, would follow them. A brooding stillness overhung the earth, broken only by the buzzing of countless insects, and the occasional scream of a robber jay.

Only the ants toiled busily, impervious to heat, and, it seemed, incapable of feeling tired. Throughout the day they toiled up and down the stems of plants and shrubs, seeking out the aphides with their honey-like excrement. The ants coaxed the aphides to produce this substance with caressing strokes of their antennae, carrying it back to the giant mound of pine needles and dried fragments of bracken that was their citadel. Other ants collected the oily seeds of the broom and gorse, which had been catapulted far from the parent plant as the pods had burst in the hot June sun. Other ants foraged for what they could find, a fragment of a dead earthworm, a tiny green caterpillar, a legless grasshopper.

The first wasps flew swiftly under the trees, hunting down the flies which droned around in their search for carrion. Swift though the flies were, they were no match for the striped yellow hunter that flew among them with snapping pincers and fatal sting. The fly would be seized, stung, and carried to the ground, where the wasp would remove wings, legs, and antennae, before rising with difficulty and labouring back to the nest with its bounty, food for the carnivorous grubs which were to emerge in such numbers in the autumn.

At night, when the dew lay silver on the short turf of the meadows, the hermaphrodite worms would emerge to lie, each with its tail gripping its burrow, stretched and shining on the grass, seeking a mate to fertilize its eggs. The badgers, who loved these big lobworms, would leave the hills and roam many miles, moving with unusual stealth as they pounced upon the quick-moving, sensitive worms. On some nights they ate earthworms to the exclusion of all other food, but the corn was ripening, and soon one badger or another would roll in the corn, flattening it so that it could reach the succulent ears of grain. Then it would call down the wrath of the farmer on all the members of its tribe.

On such nights as these, Syla taught her kitts to hunt. They learnt quickly, faring better than their mother had done, when she had taught herself the art of hunting. The kitts at first caught mainly small fry, beetles and grubs, earthworms and little frogs, but their mother brought them half dead voles, on which they learnt to pounce and kill. They learnt too how to scent out nests of baby voles, and how to leap up in the night, to pull down foolish fledgling birds, that knew no better than to sleep in the low branches of shrubs. One night Jeta learnt a lesson she was never to forget.

The weather was dry, and the family had been pulling apart rotten tree stumps, in search of the rich bounty to be found there. Slow worms frequented such places. Great white grubs, as thick as a man's finger, juicy and succulent, lay beneath the rotten bark. Snails clustered in the moist grass at the foot of the stump, and often a mouse would scamper out of the debris.

The family had demolished one stump as far as they were able, being less expert at the task than badgers, and were about to move on when Jeta noticed a slight movement in the soft dust. She dug down, and chittered to the others to advertise her find, but the two males looked back, bored with Jeta, and her excavations, and anxious to explore fresh fields. Only Syla realized what Jeta had found, having spotted it herself in their foraging. She screamed a warning, but either it came too late, or else Jeta paid no heed.

As the toad burrowed further down into the soft wood dust, Jeta seized it in her jaws, and instantly the toxins from the toad's warty poison glands sprayed into her mouth, scalding and searing her gums and tongue. Instantly Jeta released the toad, which retired unhurt, while Jeta rolled in agony, foaming at the mouth and rubbing her face with frantic front paws.

Gradually the pain wore off, so that by morning she was free of discomfort. She did not feed again that night and confined herself to drinking copious draughts of water. She never touched another toad.

With the kitts to assist her at fishing, Syla learnt to catch the sea trout that arrived in the salmon pool. Remorselessly they would harry the great fish from corner to corner of the pool, never letting it rest until chance, or a mistake on the part of the fish, delivered it to the waiting jaws of one of the mink. Then, as the struggling fish towed its captor round the pool, the others would join in the kill and gradually wear it down. Sometimes the buffeting the mink received in these struggles made the game seem hardly worth while, so they did not hunt the sea trout every night, but went for easier prey. Only occasionally, and then more for sport than to satisfy their hunger, did

Syla and her kitts harass the sea trout. Many more went up river from the pool than were killed.

Now there were more sea trout in the river than it would comfortably hold. As the waters grew warmer and held less oxygen the disease latent in the fish flared up, and great weals and blisters appeared on the flaccid flanks of those fish longest in the river. In the overcrowded pools the disease spread quickly, and one by one the fish died and floated silently back down to the sea, or were caught and held, shining white crescents, wedged belly up among the stones. There were too many fish in the river, but the riparian owners would not allow anyone to fish for them, only a favoured few, and the law dealt heavily with poachers.

Now that the kitts had grown so big and active, the family roamed further and further afield. Long before twilight the impatient kitts were clamouring to be away, and dawn found them still hunting, often far away from the old nest in the log. They took to spending days and nights away from the nesting site, working their way far downstream, or exploring tiny tributaries which led them high up into the hills. They followed the stream where Syla had lived before she found the river, and went past the farm where Motik had met his death.

Here they came to the marsh field, and found a rich new hunting ground among the reeds and sedges. The river here was sluggish and winding, with deep pools under the steep, overhanging banks, and the trout were unused to being hunted. Here too the mink found many eels, frogs, newts, and insects. They found a mallard with a late brood of young, a dozen speckled ducklings with fragments of egg shell still clinging to their downy backs. The mink killed and ate all but two, which the mother led away upriver, on a long and arduous walk overland, which lasted all one night.

The mink kitts sampled all kinds of strange fare, including water snails, which were particularly abundant here. One of the snails carried a tiny parasite, a fluke, which was to migrate to Bara's liver, and cause his death some six months later.

No crops grew on this marsh. No sheep or cattle were allowed to graze here because of the fluke. The river was lost at times amid forests of green irises, and the heather and wortleberries grew in great woody clumps among tussocks of reed. The slobbery ground spongy under its carpet of green and gold lichen, was always waterlogged, the breeding ground of countless midges and mosquitoes, and here grew the strange sundew, with its sticky petals spread to trap the unwary flies. In the twisting, winding channels that interlaced the marsh, many creatures lived and died. Snipe and curlew probed the soft earth with their long bills. Water vole and shrew scurried secretively to and fro, half hidden from the watching eyes of sparrow hawk, kestrel and buzzard. Grass snakes and adders lay twined among the twisted branches of the heather, numerous small brown birds, warblers and buntings, pipits and chiffchaffs, lived their short and furtive, secret lives here. Here Ispi had raised a family, in a disused martin's nest in a bank, and here an ancient dog otter lived, one paw crippled from the iron jaws of a trap, from which he had bitten free. Here, too, was a small colony of rabbits, in defiance of disease and rabbit clearance societies.

The marsh was a favourite haunt of Arda, the heron, for here he could rely on being well out of gunshot range from any angle. Here he came when the wind blew too strong in the estuary, or when the tide was too full. He came one dull morning, before the light was bright enough for him to see fish, and stood, a grey emaciated shadow, his scaly grey legs at one with the phalanx of reeds around him. Only his eyes, yellow and glittering, with their pupils of jet black, betrayed his presence. For an hour he stood, as if carved from slate.

The mink were hunting through the reeds, well scattered, and comparatively silent. The heron heard them, but could not see them. He stayed where he was, his deadly rapier of a beak resting on his chest, waiting.

Jeta was on the left flank, six feet away from Syla. Kiva hung behind, investigating the half chewed reeds that lay where a water vole had hastily abandoned his meal. Bara pounded in vain pursuit of a water hen which was now a hundred yards away, still clucking noisily and telling itself how lucky it had been to escape.

The light was stronger now, and the cleave was black against the sun, its top shrouded in mist and its base discreetly petticoated with a sombre frill of oaks. A crow called, far out in the distant morning, once, twice, thrice; a lonely sound, brooding over the stillness and silence of the marsh. Jeta heard the crow, and then the morning was no more, as Arda drove his bill down, through the base of her skull and into the muddy water below her.

As the life went out she kicked, once, although she was already dead, and the splash, together with the movement of the heron, alerted Syla and brought her flashing, white hot with fear and anger, through the shrouding curtain of reeds. Arda was in the act of throwing Jeta's corpse into the air, in order to catch it again, and swallow it, as Syla sprang at his upraised throat. Arda squawked, and then dropped the dead kitt, as he spread his wings to try and rise. Kiva arrived, in answer to Syla's scream, and flung himself at one wildly flapping vane.

The blow from the heron's wing almost knocked him senseless, but his teeth closed on the bony pinion joint, and he hung on, feeling himself flung to and fro, as with eyes closed he sank his teeth deeper and deeper, and waited patiently for the buffeting to cease.

The heron floundered away, his head sinking as Syla's weight dragged it down, but before he had gone more than a pace or two Bara, attracted by the commotion, had arrived. Seeing a scaly grey foot upraised, Bara grabbed, felt bone and sinew crack between his jaws, and then found himself forced down into the water and mud. Releasing his hold, he grabbed the wing which threatened to hurl his brother into thin air, and he too obtained a grip near the joint.

Arda stabbed sideways, missing Syla but catching Bara, severing an ear, and laying bare the skin on Bara's neck. Bara flung himself at the blood-engorged eye above the slashing beak, and Arda screamed as the mink's teeth sank into his face, and two scrabbling paws clawed at his eye. Slowly, under the combined weight of the mink, he sank down into the frothy bloodstained water. One wing and one leg were useless, and the weight of Bara stopped him using his bill. He closed his eyes, sank slowly into the water, and drowned as Syla bit into the arteries of his tough and stringy neck.

Of Jeta's body there was no sign. It had drifted away downstream, to be found by a buzzard later in the day. The mink left Arda where he lay, having no wish to eat the rancid, stringy flesh, and later the crows found him, and pecked out his eyes. Other animals and insects flocked to the feast, and soon there was no trace of Arda, save for his skull, with its long bill, growing like a petrified reed among the green.

After this tragedy Syla and her two sons moved on, drifting back downstream, past the salmon pool and the woodland, hardly recognizing the hollow log, until at last they came to the end of the cleave, and into the fair green pastures of the valley.

# 16 The Parting of the Ways

SYLA did not stay long in the lowlands. The proximity of man, the barking of his dogs, the clatter and whirr of his machinery, unsettled and unnerved her, making her restless and uneasy. The scenes and accompanying sounds recalled vague long-forgotten fragments of memory, of times associated with her captivity and early days of freedom, days in which she had not been conscious of unhappiness, but which now assumed the proportions of nightmare. For two days the trio travelled downstream, passing the entrance of another tributary. Here Syla wanted to turn off, but the brothers ignored her chirrups of invitation, and now Syla followed her kitts. They were too big to bully, and too independent.

On the second night they passed under a bridge by a small town, where a mill wheel clattered and groaned, and by dawn the trio stood at the junction of their river with another far greater than they had ever seen. Here the water was sluggish and deep, with shoals of dace and red-finned roach co-existing with the trout and salmon parr. Bream cruised in massive shoals, stirring up the mud as they grubbed for bloodworms and chironomid larvae. The water tasted brackish, flat, devoid of life and oxygen. Much of it had been abstracted from the river, used in tens of thousands of homes, and then returned purified as well as possible from its contaminating cargo of sewage and industrial toxins.

Syla explored the river for about a mile downstream, but found that it did not improve. She caught a dace, but the large tough scales caught at her throat, making her retch and cough. Dawn was breaking over the estuary, and the waters of the river were pink and oily in the translucent light. A cormorant flew past, heading upriver with rapid wingbeats and arrow-straight flight. A magpie chattered, and as if in answer a thin breeze stirred the grasses that grew thick by the river bank, making them shiver in the early morning air. Syla turned away and called softly to the kitts.

Kiva had caught an eel, and he and Bara lay in shallow water, one eating the head, one chewing the tail. When they met in the middle there would be a squabble, with much baring of teeth and harmless butting of heads. At the moment they were at peace with each other, and ignored their mother. Syla called again, this time more imperiously, and at that moment a chance event settled matters beyond the control of the mink.

Out of the mists of the morning there came a dull roar, which grew rapidly to a nerve-shattering cacophony of sound. Over and above the metallic clanking and din of pounding machinery came the hideous two tone blare of a horn, and the mink panicked and fled in all directions as an early morning diesel train thundered along the track beside the river. Syla eventually stopped running in a drainage ditch fifty yards from the river, and laid low, her heart thudding and her limbs trembling, for over half an hour. When she emerged it was full daylight. She never saw her kitts again.

At the approach of the train, Kiva and Bara had dived, to resurface fifty yards downstream. For several hours they lost touch with each other, and when they met they were both too tired to do more than crawl into a hollow beneath some pollard willows, and sleep until dusk. In the months that were to follow, they remained inseparable, and enjoyed some notoriety through their exploits. They appeared one Sunday in broad daylight, and were pursued by a group of anglers who were holding a fishing match. They penetrated to the heart of a town and killed the goldfish in an ornamental pond. They raided a chicken run, killing three pullets and wounding many more. They were sighted many times, and since they were always on the move, and since one black mink looked exactly like any other, reports were put about that a great plague of the creatures had invaded the valley. Many traps were set, which caught rats, stoats, an old ferret which had been living wild for many months, and a female mink which had escaped from a farm only a fortnight previously.

Gradually the flukes that had invaded the liver of Bara began to have their effect. Now the difference between the two brothers grew more apparent, as Kiva grew sleeker and fatter, whilst Bara became thin and haggard, with a dull, staring coat. As the anaemia took its toll, Bara grew slower, less agile, less eager to hunt, and one cold morning in December he crawled into a tree root with Kiva and fell asleep, never to awake. Kiva tried several times to rouse him in the purple dusk, until at last, growling, with hackles raised, Kiva backed away from this strange still thing that looked like, but was not, his brother. By morning he was three miles away, with the salt wind in his face, and the rolling tides and the mudflats of the estuary before him. Here he was to stay, to meet a female mink, and to raise several families, but his story, and the details which surrounded it, is lost among the nodding sea pinks and the marram grass of the dunes.

Any regret that Syla may have felt at the loss of her kitts was soon dispelled by the light-hearted freedom that absolved her from all sense of duty. The relief that came with the passing of responsibility, and the lessening of nervous tension sent her running and playing, back upriver to the wild country she knew so well. For a while she took a holiday, and explored the tributary that had caught her attention on the journey downstream. Here she found new pools to explore, and the trout were easy victims to her practised jaws. Higher and higher she climbed, following a steep valley where the trees grew so thickly that the river never saw the sky. Moss and ferns grew thickly in the damp and shade, and a hundred tiny rivulets trickled down through the rocks and shale.

She came at last to the wide moor, where no trees grew, and the wind blew unceasingly, susurring eternally through the dry grasses and bent heather stems. The river ended in a bog, a quaking mire of mosses and peat, with patches of clear blue water which was cold and totally devoid of life. Crossing this, Syla came again to another river, flowing away down the opposite side of the hill. Syla journeyed on, not realizing that she had come upon the source of her own river, where she had passed the previous winter, and raised her family of kitts. So she came back to the cleave, and the woodland pool, and Arak the raven noted her arrival, as he noted all things, croaking his hatred from the wind-bitten thorn that grew by the tor.

Syla soon settled into her old ways, hunting and fishing through nights which grew appreciably longer with each setting sun. Now salmon mingled with the sea trout that lay in the pools, great svelte fish glowing deeply dusky pink against the gold of the gravel. Syla harried the salmon, and once took a great bite out of the tail of one. For her pains she was flung across the river, dashed against a rock, and surfaced twenty yards downstream, bruised and half drowned, narrowly escaping being swept down the rapids.

There came a succession of rainy, gusty days, with the river running high and dirty with silt. Syla, driven away from the river, hunted through the rain-drenched fern and waterlogged pastures, killing and eating anything she could find, but often returning, cold and hungry to a new lie she had found where a dry stone wall ran down to the river. With the coming of the new moon the weather changed, the wind blowing from the east and bringing a succession of dry fine days, which would have been hot but for the cooling breeze.

Now the river was full of small summer peal, young sea trout which had followed their earlier, larger brethren to the spawning grounds. As the river dropped the trout ceased their journeying and lay locked in the pools, spending the day like grey shadows under the shade of the alders, and by night feeding on the white moths that flitted out of the alders. Syla took several of these small sea trout, eating as much of the creamy pink flesh as she could manage, and leaving the remains, rather tactlessly, for anyone to find. Each night the moon grew in stature and brilliance, and each fresh dawn saw another silver corpse half eaten on sand or gravel bar.

Still the rivers, impoverished by abstraction and dulled by pollution of many kinds, held too many fish, and time and again a sea trout, weakened by the strain and battering from the long journey through white water and rough granite, exhausted from leaping over weir and dam, poisoned by the toxins which seeped into the river from towns with outdated, overloaded sewage systems, arrived at the head waters, only to turn over on its side, flopping feebly, its sight dimmed and its balance gone, its frayed gills tormented and destroyed, to be borne away by the river. Thus perished unborn generations of sea trout, so that in time to come, of the proud legions that once lashed every river in the land to white foam with the frenzy of their passing, there would be too few to carry on the fight, and the unknown hunters of the sea would end what man had begun.

Many creatures, animals and birds, flocked to the feast of dead and dying fish. Fox and badger, rats, magpies, crows, herring gulls, buzzards, and, of course, Arak the raven, all scavenged along the river bank in search of this bounty of flesh. What remained was quickly cleared, by countless lesser individuals, and here and there the maggots from rotting fish dropped back into the river, once more to feed the living. Some fed too well, and small trout died, their gills choked by a surfeit of the wriggling white grubs.

At the time of the full moon, strangers arrived on the cleave. They came by night, stepping daintily along the twisting badger tracks among the tall nodding fern that hid them from view. For over a year they had wandered, drifting down through Somerset, crossing over Exmoor, following the wooded banks of the rivers through Devon, into the thickly forested hills, with their regimented ranks of thick fir, and so into the foothills of the moor. The roe deer were small and secretive, travelling by night and hiding by day, preferring to shelter in thicket and tall bracken rather than to flee when danger threatened, so that they could hide in a good sized garden without being noticed. The buck carried a pair of short, wickedly pointed antlers, and the doe led twin fawns.

Syla noticed their droppings, here and there in the woods, but it was some time before she met the family face to face. Then one dusk, as she ran down the path by the river, she came upon the deer as they stood drinking. At her approach the doe turned, crashing away through the bracken, and followed by her fawns, but the buck stood his ground, facing Syla and cutting the turf with impetuous strokes of one dainty hoof.

Syla was used to sheep, and in her experience they always stampeded away at her approach. She was thus a trifle nonplussed at the unusual behaviour of this remarkably sheeplike animal, and so, chittering with anger at being barred from access to the river, she attempted to pass. At once the buck wheeled in front of her, swinging his head low and scything the grass blades with his horns. In sudden fury Syla flew at his muzzle, moving so quickly that the buck had no time to impale her, and the next moment Syla's teeth were sunk deep in the cartilage of his nose.

Syla could not hold her grip for long, and as she fell away she saw the buck rear high into the air, and saw his twin hooves, their edges sharp and keen, cutting down to trample her. With a scream, she dodged aside, but failed to notice that she was close against a small granite rock. For a moment her movements were checked, and as she recovered, one hoof grazed down her shoulder. Her left foreleg and paw, which otherwise would have been pressed harmlessly into soft earth, was crushed and skinned against the rough granite of the rock, the blood showing darkly wet against the stone.

As the buck rose again to strike, Syla slipped beneath him, diving headlong into the river. Here she drifted steadily downstream until she could safely clamber ashore. The buck returned to his family, and Syla limped painfully back along the path to her home in the dry stone wall. Here she lay for the remainder of the night, whimpering as the mangled limb began to throb and burn, until at dawn her fever and thirst drove her out to drink at the riverside.

Three days passed, and Syla knew no difference between daylight and dark. She emerged only to drink, having no hunger, and being quite unable to make more than a slow, limping progress that was a mere travesty of her former grace. She had lost a lot of blood. Her leg was swollen and purple, with a great tear running down her forearm. One toe was missing completely, and the bones of her wrist were broken.

Arak the raven noticed her plight as she made her way to the waterside at dawn, as he had noticed the coming of the roe, and the blood smears on the granite rock. Now he haunted the riverside, waiting for Syla to reappear. For several days he hung about the woodland, and it was as if his presence laid a blight upon every living creature. At his approach, birds and animals hid or fled, but Arak was content to pick a meagre living from lizards and beetles. He had spent his life waiting as he waited now, and he had never been wrong.

# 17 The Change

YET in the end Arak was to be cheated of his prey, for on the fifth night, as an ochre moon hung low over the ripening land, Syla crawled out of the dry stone wall, and, obeying some strange impulse born of delirium, dragged herself along the river bank, back to the log where she had given birth to her kitts. Slowly she was losing the battle to survive, and the ultimate foe, the organism which was to rob her of life, was not even an animal, but a lowly form of vegetable.

Inside her wrist, among the warm decaying debris of shattered bone and blood vessel, a small group of bacteria, carried into the wound on a plug of hair and skin, were growing and multiplying. The staphylococci grew at a phenomenal rate. Every thirty minutes they would split in half, forming two new individuals where once there was but one. At first they were few in number, and the white corpuscles of Syla's blood fell upon them, digesting and destroying them almost as fast as they could reproduce.

Gradually, however, the bacteria gained in numbers and vigour. The wound was too great, and the bodily defences too scattered, while the patrolling forces of the blood were impeded by the damage to the surrounding tissues. Gradually the invading bacteria spread through the limb, into the bloodstream, coming to rest and reproducing throughout Syla's body. They lodged in the lymph nodes, in the lungs and kidneys, and eventually they came to the lining of Syla's heart.

Death was very close to Syla now, hovering down with rushing black wings as if impatient to lead her away into the dark maw of nothing. Yet still Syla fought back, rallying and returning to brief moments of consciousness, in which she embraced the familiar hard objects she had gathered as her playthings so many months ago. For a short while she would lie, her breathing harsh and laboured, staring into the darkness and waiting stoically for whatever might befall her.

She felt no pain, only the burning of the fever that raged in an effort to destroy the bacteria which poured their toxins into her system. She felt thirsty, and drifted into a strange dream world in which she swam through water as black as night. The water flowed silkily past her flanks, until a great silver sea trout swept towards her, a fish which became a roaring, clattering diesel train, thundering along in the pale light of early dawn. Then the dawn turned to red fire, and the flames licked the cleave in the dusk of a spring night, while from the sky pheasants fell, to lie flopping like galleons, stranded, shipwrecked on some sandy shore.

Syla fell upon the pheasant, but it turned into a white

terrier, lying on its side and scrabbling at the rocks which held it firm. Then the world was filled with white light, and she was floating, flying through the air, faster and faster, until she could look down and see the cleave and the woodlands below her, split by the shining silver ribbon of the river. The moon shone brighter, and the stars glowed like orange balls of fire. Then they too faded, and Syla was lost in an indigo blue bowl of night, waiting for a dawn which never came.

Syla's body lay on a couch of soft, dry grass, entombed in the hollow log, and the river flowed softly by. Day followed night, and autumn came, then winter. The seasons ebbed and flowed. All seemed as permanent and endless as the rocks of the cleave, yet even they were finite. Moss grew on the hollow log, and graceful ferns filled the hollow where once Syla and her kitts were seen playing in the soft summer nights. Slowly the log mouldered and crumbled into the earth, and the substance that was once the living, graceful body of Syla changed back into the elements, the calcium and the iron, the iodine and the cobalt, the phosphorus and the manganese, all the numerous minerals and salts, the gases and liquids from which she was made. The warm earth reclaimed them, for the land does not give up her riches, but merely lends them to those who know best how to use them, as she has ever done, and always will.

But what of the life that was Syla? What had become of the tiny white flame that had burnt so brightly for so brief a while, that had known freedom and hunger, passion in the embrace of Motik, love for her kitts, and anger and hatred against her enemies? Would it be reborn in the daughters of Kiva, or ring clear as crystal in the song of an unborn skylark? Would it lie imprisoned in the scent of the wild hyacinth, changed by the earth through some chemistry as yet unknown to us? These are secrets which lie hidden in the flowers of the moss; whispered by the wind that blows through the brooding oaks.

Syla knew but a tiny fragment of life, of the great pattern which lies spread across the loom of the land. Once there was no warp or weft, and though the centuries tick by, second by second, the design still grows. And it is ever changing, ever new, although the basic design is the same. The legions of life that are passed have, in dying, made room and substance available for the new, and so life will go on, until the sun is but a tiny star on the far horizon, and the world revolves in endless night, locked in a pall of ice.

The secret that was Syla lies locked in the earth from whence it came, the earth which holds uncounted similar secrets, and perhaps it is as well that no key is to be found. It never occurred to Syla to ask why, to wonder why she was born, or to consider why she had to spend her brief life in an alien soil, or what purpose her short existence served in the weaving of the great carpet of life. She lived and died in obedience to the wishes of a force far greater than she, following blindly the instructions that led her to her destiny.

The impact of her existence, and that of her kind, was so small as to be almost insignificant. Yet the interwoven threads that linked her with her environment are so cunningly intermingled with those of other lives that it would be possible, given the ability, to trace connecting links between the life of Syla, and the fate of a mammal like the great blue whale, even now swimming on a course which will lead inevitably to extinction. All this is permanently written in the pattern of evolution. The individual dies in obedience to the race, and the species dies, to make way for newer, changing forms of life. Throughout the sifting, changing sands of time, this alone is constant, and it seems that no matter how the pattern may change, one thing is certain. Somewhere in the great wheel of the universe, there will always be life.

## ABOUT THE AUTHOR

Ewan Clarkson was born in 1929 in Cumberland, spent his childhood in Cheshire, and has since lived in Bath, Southampton, and Epping Forest, before moving to Devon. Most of the time he lived in a caravan and has spent his life keeping and studying animals and learning about the countryside.

He has had many jobs, including zoo-keeping and mink farming, but makes his living mainly by writing articles and short stories, mainly about animals, angling and the country scene. He lived for a while in a lonely house on Dartmoor, where he wrote *Break for Freedom*, and now lives in a thatched cottage with his wife and two children beside the river Teign, two miles from the estuary and eight from the moor. He has been many years in Devon but is still 'slightly overwhelmed with the beauty and wealth of the country' that surrounds him.

Mr Clarkson's other book is *Halic, the Story of a Grey Seal*, published by Hutchinson.

*Some other Puffins you might enjoy*

## BRADY

*Jean Fritz*

'It was an Underground Railroad station,' said Brady. 'I saw it with my own eyes. Over by Drover Hull's. He's got two runaway slaves over there.'

But Brady knew before he finished that he had made a blunder. The room went very quiet, then everyone started to talk at once about everything under the sun except the organization which helped slaves escape to freedom in Canada.

From then on, Brady was involved in the slavery question, and forced to take sides. More important still, he learned to keep a secret, when he discovered that one slip of his tongue could betray his own father.

For readers of eleven and over.

## THE BATTLEFIELD

*William Mayne*

The Battlefield was in Yorkshire. It was a piece of waste land lying above the road to the moors, full of trees and soft ground. No one knew who had fought there; some said it was the Irish, some the Romans, and Debby thought it was probably people in the Civil War. There were tales that the beck sometimes ran red with blood, and ghostly lights were sometimes seen at night.

Most people preferred to leave it well alone, but Lesley and Debby loved exploring there. Then one day they saw the beck really run red and began finding strange objects, and all the grown-ups got interested as well.

For readers of nine and over.

## MAGIC BY THE LAKE

*Edward Eager*

'Have you noticed the name on the cottage?' asked Katharine. She and the rest of her family had just arrived at their holiday cottage.

'Magic by the Lake,' said Martha. 'Doesn't it sound lovely? Don't you wish it were true?'

Then Mark's turtle stuck its head out of its shell. 'Now you've done it,' it said. 'You couldn't be sensible, could you, and order magic by the pound, for instance, or by the day? Or by threes, the good old fashioned way? You had to be greedy and order magic by the lake, and of course now you've got a whole lakeful of it!'

Readers of *Half Magic* will already know Mr Eager's particular blend of enchantment, with its mixture of humour, wild adventure, and everyday happenings.

## TARKA THE OTTER

*Henry Williamson*

This story of an otter is as true as long observations and keen insight could make it. It lets you live with Tarka and see at his level (much closer to the ground than our eye level) the wild life of that stretch of Devon country which runs from Dartmouth to the sea, between the rivers Torridge and Taw. With a good map you can follow almost every step of the story.

To read Tarka for the first time is a tremendous experience whatever your age. It would be a pity to try it too young, but most people over ten will enjoy it.

## SATURDAY AND THE IRISH AUNT

*Jenifer Wayne*

Jessica, Nonnie and Ben had never met their grandfather while he was alive, and certainly didn't expect his will to be interesting – but they were wrong, for he had left each of them fifty pounds, *to spend exactly as they liked.*

Fifty pounds each! It was odd that in spite of their excitement they could think of so few practical ways of spending it that were neither too big nor too small. Jessica was bursting with schemes, like starting a pottery or building a theatre, and Ben was torn between ideas of modernizing his bedroom, motorbikes, and buying a cow. And Nonnie? She was in the worst dilemma of all, she had to choose between the lonely pony she longed to buy and saving grandfather's poor old mare in Ireland.

And then, as if the excitement wasn't already at boiling point, their Irish Aunt arrived.

For readers of nine and over.

## THE GOALKEEPER'S REVENGE AND OTHER STORIES

*Bill Naughton*

Here are thirteen stories, some dramatic, some thrilling, and some even sad, but all about boys. The boys who fish, fight and play football, race their four-wheeled trolleys, go into hospital, apply for their first job.

Bill Naughton's imagination and skill make this book a real breakthrough in storytelling for young readers of eleven and over.

## MY SIDE OF THE MOUNTAIN

*Jean George*

'I am on my mountain in a tree home that people have passed without ever knowing I am here. The house is a hemlock tree six feet in diameter. I came upon it last summer and dug and burnt it out until I made a snug home in the tree.

'My bed is on the right. On the left is a small fireplace with a chimney that leads the smoke out through a knothole. It snowed all day yesterday and today. It must be below zero outside, and yet I can sit here inside my tree and write with bare hands. It is the fourth of December, I think. It is eight months since I ran away from home.'

This is part of Sam Gribley's diary. Sam had escaped from his family's cramped flat in New York and his eight brothers and sisters to live on the barren farm his grandfather had owned in the Catskill Mountains. He had a pen-knife, an axe, a ball of string, and some flint and steel, and that was all.

## PONIES PLOT

*C. Northcote Parkinson*

The world is full of books about ponies, written for children. This is completely different, a book about children, written for ponies. Instead of the child teaching the pony how to jump – as if it didn't *know* – it is the pony who teaches the child how to ride.

From a pony's point of view, all riding schools have the same thing wrong with them: they are for children who *can't* ride. As soon as a child becomes bearable, she vanishes and has a pony of her own, and her place is taken by another. The newcomers are certain to scream when the pony walks and as likely to fall off as soon as it comes to a halt. 'Here we go again,' the ponies grumble, and who can blame them?

So under Old Smokey's tuition, the ponies each decided what sort of girl they would like and how they were to train and discipline her when they had her.

If you have enjoyed this book and would like to know about others which we publish, why not join the Puffin Club? You will be sent the Club magazine *Puffin Post* four times a year and a smart badge and membership book. You will also be able to enter all the competitions. Write for details to:

The Puffin Club Secretary
Penguin Books
Bath Road
Harmondsworth
Middlesex